ALEXIS

ALIEN SURROGATE AGENCY #3

TASHA BLACK

13TH STORY PRESS

13th Story Press

PO Box 506

Swarthmore, PA 19081

13thStoryPress@gmail.com

Cover designed by Sylvia Frost of The Book Brander

TASHA BLACK STARTER LIBRARY

Packed with steamy shifters, mischievous magic, alien
adventures, billionaire superheroes, and plenty of HEAT,
the Tasha Black Starter Library is the perfect way to dive
into Tasha's unique brand of Romance with Bite!
Get your FREE books now at tashablack.com!

ALEXIS

1

———

ALEXIS

Alexis Clare tightened her torso and pulled up from her belly, willing her spine to lengthen slightly so she could add speed to her spin.

The music began to swell, the beats coming faster and faster as it built to a crescendo.

She extended her leg and quickly swept it in again. The movement was rhythmic and mesmerizing, but its real job was to speed up the turn and maintain her momentum for the next one, giving her audience the impression that she was in effortless, perpetual motion.

In reality, there was a whole lot of effort involved. But onstage, it was the dancer's job to make it look easy.

Her arms opened and tightened with perfect timing to add to her speed. Even her eyes had to remain on a precise spot at the back of the theater, her head whipping around crisply to find it again at the end of each turn, so that she wouldn't become disoriented and lose her place on the stage.

The Black Swan included thirty-two of the dizzying fouetté turns in a row. The secret, though, was that dizziness was the least of your problems, as long as you spotted properly with your eyes.

The real danger was the difficulty of staying up *en pointe* while keeping the hips perfectly level through every single whip-quick spin, all while pulling up, and employing the arms for speed and beauty, and spotting, and, of course, smiling like it was all effortless, thirty-two times.

Alexis was almost there. She could taste that last turn, hear the sweet sound of the applause already breaking in her mind.

But the ghost of a twinge in her ankle pulled her instantly out of the fantasy.

Distracted by the expectation of pain, she let one hip lift slightly as she extended her leg and immediately lost her balance, nearly crashing to the floor on her twenty-seventh turn.

So much for that applause.

"Stop simulation," she called out.

The stage, the velvet curtains, and the auditorium beyond disappeared, leaving her back in the plain gymnasium of the Midsummer Fertility Center on Maltaffia.

Alexis had been here for a week now, waiting for her match to arrive.

It was good in many ways to have a little time to lick her wounds before she got back on the horse.

It seemed like over the last two years, her charmed life had swiftly lost a lot of its charm.

She had grown up in the city on Terra-58, a beautiful planet with every modern convenience, as well as gorgeous green spaces planned and planted generously during terraforming.

When she fell in love with ballet, her father had signed

her up for training in the ancient Terran art. She quickly abandoned everything else in her life to follow the dream.

She left school and took courses online in the corridors of the Great Theater. Her only friends were dancers. She lived to push herself harder, to make wild demands of her mind and body.

Growing up in the darkened theater, she learned about the world from the stories of the old ballets, which described a life so different from the world of Terra-58 that it hardly bore comparison.

Love would be the same in any circumstance, though, or so it seemed.

Her father lost his job, but by then she had a position in the company and trained for free. She even received a salary that was just enough to share an apartment with three other dancers and pay for the healthy food she needed to keep up with the demands of her art. It wasn't much. But it was all she needed.

Then came the ankle injury.

It happened onstage, when she was dancing a soloist's role in a performance of Cinderella.

She wrapped the ankle and danced the rest of the performance, then went to the company doctor.

It took months for the ankle to heal enough for her to dance on. And it was so tender, she could hardly stand it.

The doc assured her it would heal just fine with time. But the kiss of death to a dance career was to be *injury prone,* so she got back to the barre the day she was allowed, and worked through the pain.

Late at night, icing the swollen joint, she researched how to reduce the pain. Weight loss was highly recommended for overweight patients.

Though she was already an athlete, and anything but

overweight, the idea was compelling. Less weight would also make her easier to partner. She would be more likely to be promoted to principal if she were even lighter than she was.

That was the beginning of a downward spiral.

The ankle hurt, she cut her calories, she was low in energy, she was sloppy and forgot to baby the ankle, it hurt again, she cut her food intake, and on and on it went.

Her father would never have allowed it if he had been there to see, but by then, he had moved out to a low-cost suburb to start over.

By the end of the season, she was haggard, hobbled, and haunted. And the company doctor told her that she was being pulled for six months to rest the ankle.

It was a big blow, and it was tough to take. But she had one more thing driving her. The last light in her heart was the idea of finding true love. Every single ballet she had ever performed in ended either with a happily ever after or with a tragedy of lost love.

But on Terra-58, if a woman wanted to be eligible for marriage, she had to first produce a primary heir. This was done with the help of a fertility clinic.

Alexis had always been too focused on her dance to worry much about all that. So maybe this was a blessing in disguise. She decided to spend the time she was benched from ballet working on having a baby so she could start that other part of her life.

But from the very first appointment at the clinic, she learned she had destroyed that hope, too. A restricted diet coupled with extreme exercise meant she hadn't experienced her monthly in a year. And that meant no babies.

Meetings with a nutritionist came next. She watched her body fill out enough to bleed again.

And though she was scared at times that she might

never dance again, the return of her nutritional health brought back her positive outlook.

Suddenly, though things were worse than ever on paper, she was beginning to *feel* better.

But then her first fertility procedure didn't work. Neither did the second. And that was the end of her meager savings.

At the end of the six months, the doctors did more scans and determined that her ankle was physically sound - as strong as before, maybe stronger after all the physical therapy.

She went back to dance for the company, in the corps now instead of as a soloist. And she took a second job at a grocery store stocking shelves overnight to save for a final treatment.

And that one failed too.

But Alexis had always been a positive, motivated person. Instead of letting the bad news drag her back to hell, she decided to relax for a day or two and spend as much time as possible in the park, brainstorming what to do next.

Then her friend, Haven, from the fertility support group feeds, told her about a special opportunity - an agency that would match her with a man from another planet who wanted a child.

His seed would *awaken her womb*, whatever that meant, and she would bear him a baby. She would be paid handsomely, and on her return home, her own treatments would be more effective from the interspecies encounter. It all sounded like a bunch of non-scientific nonsense to her, but science hadn't gotten her too far up to that point.

The only downside was that certain species required a physical mating act and even the use of the surrogate's eggs as a donor as well as a surrogate.

As soon as Haven finished telling her about it, Alexis

was on the hush rail with her medical files loaded up on her bracelet.

She never would have imagined agreeing to such a thing a year ago.

But the more time she spent in the real world, outside of the theater, the more she realized she wanted to be a mother.

Children played in the park, sang in the schoolyards, ran up and down the city streets asking their parents for ice cream money.

Their joy reminded her of her own happy childhood, and the simplicity of life in those days.

A child was no longer a means to an end for her.

Now it was the end goal. It meant everything. She didn't even care about finding a love match anymore.

She was determined to have a child.

And assuming the child would want to eat, she needed to nail these turns so that she could take a larger role at the company.

"Would you like to go again," a voice seemed to come from all around her, snapping her out of her thoughts and back to the present.

"One more time," she called out. "From the turns."

"Are you certain?" The voice was so perfectly modulated it almost sounded real.

The more time Alexis spent with Oberon, the AI who had designed the Midsummer Fertility Center and who ran its immense programming, the more she had begun to consider him almost a friend.

It wasn't like she had anyone else here. And he certainly understood better than anyone else could what she was going through.

She had signed an NDA when agreeing to come. And

her friends who were already in the program were seldom able to send a comm.

"My ankle doesn't really hurt," she told him. "It was just a twinge. Like a ghost of a pain."

"I understand the concept of pain," Oberon said. "But I have never experienced it. What you are describing sounds like an echo in programming, when data is stored in its original form in one place and a copy resides elsewhere as a back-up, unused."

"So, I felt a *reference* to my actual pain, but not the pain itself," Alexis said thoughtfully. "Yeah, that's actually pretty close."

"But if you felt no pain, then why did you adjust the angle of your left hip by two degrees?" Oberon asked.

"Gods, you'd make an amazing choreographer," she said, shaking her head.

"I would not," Oberon said without sadness. "I understand the limitations of the human form, but not what is pleasing to watch."

"Watch enough ballets and that part is easy," she said.

"I have just watched *Afternoon of a Faun, Agon* and *Alice's Adventures in Wonderland*," Oberon said. "I do not understand further than before, but I will continue and report back to you when I have completed through *Zoraiya*, if you wish."

"You *watched* those ballets just now?" Alexis asked, incredulous.

"I downloaded streamed video of their recordings to my heart drive," Oberon said. "But the critical literature I have scanned gives me to understand that nothing matches the breathless uncertainty of a live performance."

"You can say that again," Alexis said ruefully. "That's how I hurt my ankle in the first place."

"I have just received word that your match's craft has landed," Oberon said.

"Now?" Alexis asked.

Her heart began to pound. She was wearing her workout clothing and covered in a sheen of sweat. She wasn't ready to make a good impression.

"You have approximately seventeen minutes until he is off-board and ready to meet you," Oberon said.

"I'll shower and change," she told him, hoping she actually had time.

It was better that her match thought she was a little late than thinking she was smelly or careless about her appearance.

Though he would be from another planet - so she had no idea what he would consider to be beauty or ugliness. Maybe a sweaty woman in a cling suit was top-shelf where he was from.

But she would feel better if she thought she was more presentable.

Best thing I can do is build up my confidence, she told herself, heading for her suite. *It's all I've got.*

2

TIAGO

Tiago Torrn adjusted his tie again as he walked barefoot down the beach toward what he hoped was his destiny.

Though Tiago had plenty of credits to spend, he had never taken a beach vacation before. And he had seldom worn a tie.

The blasted thing seemed to be trying to choke him out. He wasn't entirely sure that a man with a neck as wide as his was even meant to wear a tie. It came up short on his button-down shirt when he compared it to how his manager's ties always looked.

"The hell with it," he muttered to himself, pausing to remove the cursed thing and shove it in his pocket. He was already carrying his socks and shoes in his hand, so why stand on ceremony with the neckwear?

And after all, he was paying for all this. Surely, the intended match could handle it if he toned down the formality slightly. It occurred to Tiago that he might even be overdressed. He had no idea what kind of outfit she might show up in.

He found himself wondering once again what she looked like.

He had only been told his match was Terran, the idea of which excited him.

Terrans were exceedingly receptive to Maltaffian matings. With any luck, he would soon have a baby in his arms, one with his massive horns and her slightly softer facial features.

Though he had started off wanting a baby for business reasons, the year he had spent waiting for a match forced him to face the truth - that he *did* want a family. And he didn't want to have to answer to a mate to get it.

Life as a professional fighter had its perks, the first of which was money, and the second was not having to work in a tiny cubicle with a hologram stream half-hypnotizing you all your life.

But he didn't have a normal schedule that could be easily coordinated with another adult's to form a life together.

And of course, there were the inevitable injuries. Even if he experienced a true mate bond with a woman, which he hadn't so far, he was fairly certain she wouldn't understand why he had to have his face punched in a couple of times each standard year.

No. It was better to do this on his own. He could afford a great nanny, any exotic pets the child might want, and if he paid for private instructors, their family of two could live on the road quite happily for the next ten years or so.

When he reached his destination at last, he let out a chuckle.

He had trained with the best, gotten to the top of his game, and traveled half a world away, only to end up standing in front of another little diner.

He had practically grown up in one just like it. Tiago's adoptive parents worked hard night and day to tend to their clients and maintain the machinery of the place.

As soon as he was old enough to hold a broom, Tiago had done the same. Not because his parents asked, but because it was how they spent their waking hours, so if he wanted to spend time with them, he had to be part of the hustle bustle.

He liked the regular customers, and the delicious smells that came from the grill. But the relentlessness of the long days and nights, especially weekends and holidays, didn't appeal at all.

Tiago had gotten his fill of *an honest day's work* by the time he was fifteen. As an adult, he learned that he would much rather exercise at the gym all day and get hit in the face once in a while than bus tables and get yelled at by transport agents when the coffee wasn't hot enough.

Besides, on Maltaffia, inheritance was strictly by genetics. Adopting a child was a true charity, as it did nothing to ease financial planning. If his parents wanted Tiago to own that diner one day, they would have to sell it to him at market value if they didn't want to bury him in gift taxes that would meet or exceed the property's worth.

The day his father explained they were going to stop maintaining the place to drive down the market value so he could afford to buy it, Tiago knew it was time to tell them the truth.

"I love you guys," he had told his dad. "And I love this place because you're in it. But it's not what I want for myself when you retire. Keep it up, and when you want to sell, get as much money as you can so you can retire in style."

"Your mother will cry to think you're going to keep getting beat up for money," his father sighed.

"Remind her that I'm the one doing the beating most of the time," Tiago said.

"I don't know if she'd like that any better," his dad admitted with a wry smile.

It was true, and Tiago could only laugh.

His dad liked to say his mom had a heart as big as the diner's biggest ten-top table. She gave out more free meals and dishwashing jobs than anyone would ever know. She knew the names of the kids and grandkids of every single regular customer. The woman was pure love, in the shape of a Maltaffian mom.

But his father had continued to keep the place up and Tiago had finally made the big leagues. It had been more than a year since he'd been home, he realized with a twinge of guilt as he pushed open the door to the diner on the beach.

Bells overhead jingled as it opened, and the savory scent of bacon and eggs instantly transported him home. This diner was neat and tidy like his parents' place. But the booths and tabletops looked brand new.

He couldn't see the fry cook in the back, but by the counter, a pretty glass case of gleaming desserts spun majestically. His mother would love to have one just like it. He made a mental note to look into surprising her.

The bells over the door jingled again, and he turned to see who it was.

The woman was clearly Terran. Her features were soft and appealing, and her head was hornless and covered in a curtain of long, dark hair that looked like it would be silky to the touch.

But she moved more like a Vystian, with an effortless grace that made her look almost as if she were floating. And her slender frame had a strength to it that he recognized as a fellow athlete.

She was far too tiny to be a fighter. But maybe she was a runner or a gymnast?

If this was his intended match, both of them being athletes would be a great icebreaker. He was about to ask her what her sport was, when she looked up at him and the question died in his throat.

Her eyes were an intense cornflower blue, framed by long, dark lashes. She gazed at him as if she were reading his soul, ignoring the beefy muscles that normally got him female attention in favor of studying his expression.

He opened his mouth and closed it again, lost in her gaze.

"Tiago," he managed to say after a moment. "I'm the, uh, perspective father."

"Alexis," she replied in a soft voice like the touch of a feather, sending a shiver of awareness down his spine. "Nice to meet you."

3

ALEXIS

Alexis tried not to smile, but she was inescapably charmed by the big, beefy Maltaffian with the muscular arms and kind eyes.

His hair was long and dark, brushing his shoulders. And his skin was a lovely russet shade, reminding her of the autumn leaf simulators in the park back on Terra-58.

She hadn't met many Maltaffians, but this one was too gigantic, his muscles too defined not to be some kind of athlete.

He was too big to be a dancer. She figured he must be either a ball player, or maybe a competitive weightlifter?

"Welcome," a woman said, stepping out from the kitchen. "I'm Dr. Oppyx. Alexis, Tiago, I'm so glad you both made it. Why don't you have a seat, and we'll begin the welcome presentation?"

The woman smiled at them warmly, her brown eyes crinkling at the corners. She was a Maltaffian with lovely, blue-toned skin that contrasted deliciously with her crisp white scrubs. But she seemed petite for the species. Though maybe that was only in comparison to Tiago, who towered over both women.

The doctor was pointing them to a banquette seat on the back wall of the diner, so Alexis and Tiago headed over together.

The covering on the booth seating looked like red vinyl, and the table in front of it had a faux-marble top. It reminded Alexis a lot of the little antique diner on Terra-58 where she had spent so many nights talking after performances with her fellow dancers. It was the only place where they could stay up all night drinking nothing but black coffee and the waitresses didn't kick them out. Just the idea of it made her feel a little more at home than before.

Tiago gestured for her to sit first.

As she did, she realized how small the seat was. She tried to move as much to the side as she could, but since the inside ended in a wall, she could only go so far.

Tiago frowned at the seat like he was about to solve a puzzle, then lowered himself in slowly. His massive size meant his big thigh was pressed to hers in spite of his obvious efforts not to squish her.

She fought the urge to close her eyes as she soaked in the heat of him and the little shiver of awareness his touch sent through her.

What is wrong with me? I just met this guy...

Dr. Oppyx lifted a disc from her pocket, and waved her hand in the air.

The lights dimmed, and a hologram of a Maltaffian woman emerged into the air above the disc.

"Welcome to the Midsummer Center for Fertility," the woman chirped with a big smile. "I'm here to tell you a little about the center and the work we'll be doing here. Let me start by saying that you are the most important part of that work."

The woman began to walk along a beach. It looked a lot like the beach at the center. Alexis had spent some time exploring it on her first day.

"A first of its kind, the entire center was uniquely designed, planned and implemented by a single AI," the woman said. "And that AI, nicknamed Oberon, will also host you throughout your stay, attending to all of your needs and ensuring the best possible environment to meet our goals. We're proud to tell you that the Midsummer Center for Fertility was denoted by the Intergalactic Physicians Association as the most conception-friendly place in the galaxy."

The women took a turn and suddenly, instead of standing among the palm trees, Alexis realized that she was in a beautiful green meadow with birdsong audible in the background.

"Each day will begin with relaxing, shared activities for surrogate and intended parent," the woman went on. "Oberon has crafted a plethora of pleasant locations to help you feel at ease and get to know each other better."

There really was a lot to do. Alexis glanced at Tiago out of the corner of her eye. He would probably be up for some hiking and other outdoor activities. That could be fun.

"Here at the Midsummer Center for Fertility, everyone has responsibilities," the woman said, her voice suddenly deeper and dead serious.

The camera dramatically zoomed in on her face.

"It's the responsibility of this clinic to ensure your safety at all times," she said. "Say the words *escape me now* at any time, and Oberon will cancel programming immediately."

Alexis bit her lip, immediately reminded of something she generally tried to repress.

Back in her younger days with the ballet company, there had been an overly passionate fan who became a stalker. He tried to grab her at the backstage door one night, and had it not been for the brave actions of one of her fellow dancers, he might have been successful.

She kept her eyes on the holo-film, determined not to think about it.

"In addition, for security and training purposes, everything that happens at the Midsummer Center for Fertility will be recorded," the woman went on. "However, if you say the words *confirm privacy mode,* Oberon will not display the proceedings to our staff."

That would be good to remember when she was showering, or if she and Tiago were supposed to get it on.

Did Maltaffians need live matings to stimulate fertility? She tried to remember if she had heard anything about them, but couldn't.

"It is the responsibility of the surrogate to submit to the necessary procedures to accomplish a pregnancy," the woman said brightly. "As a side note, according to our exit polls, 95% of participants find the procedure to be highly to extremely enjoyable."

Hmmm. So... probably yes?

She felt her cheeks heat at the idea, and hoped Tiago was watching the film and not her face.

"Upon successful conception, the surrogate will protect herself and the developing fetus by any means necessary to ensure a healthy birth," the woman was saying. "We will do all we can to ensure that the surrogate's experience is a pleasant one, however, the surrogate understands that her experience here is unique to the program. At the end of the gestational period, she will return to her home planet and there will be no further contact with the father or the offspring."

That idea was so sad that she couldn't bear to dwell on it. She pressed it down, even as she felt her heart ache at the idea of not being able to watch the child grow.

"It is the responsibility of the prospective parent to treat the surrogate with respect," the woman said sternly. "Abuse of any kind will not be tolerated. Renewed consent is required for each act of physical intimacy."

She *felt* Tiago turn to glance at her, as if checking on how she felt about what was now obvious - they were going to be making his baby the old-fashioned way.

She kept her eyes on the film and tried to keep her expression neutral. After all, she needed the money, and desperately wanted the increased fertility from this experience if she was ever going to have a child of her own, so how she felt about it didn't matter.

But she was conflicted.

Her mind was still reeling over the very real possibility that she would be leaving a baby with half her genetic materials behind with this man.

Her traitorous body was surging with eagerness to know what it was like to be wrapped in those big warm arms.

And her heart was touched that in the midst of all of this, he was checking on her, wondering if she was okay.

There was something so sweet about the big, horned man's concern. It made her feel better about everything at once. He wasn't going to hurt or abuse her. He didn't feel *entitled* to her just because she had signed a contract.

And this was an excellent first sign that he had the capacity to be a compassionate and loving parent.

"You okay?" he whispered to her.

She nodded, daring to glance up at him again.

His emerald eyes were filled with kindness, and something that looked a lot like hunger.

She wondered what he saw in hers.

4

TIAGO

Tiago fought to stay focused through the rest of the Center's presentation. But his muscles were aching for movement, and it was all he could do not to tap his feet with impatience.

He had known he would need to impregnate his match, and that there would necessarily be mating involved. But he hadn't been focused on that aspect as he thought about the process.

As a mid-level celebrity on Maltaffia, known for his good looks, he had never lacked attention from women. He had figured the female assigned to him here would be matched to him biologically, but he doubted he would actually be more than moderately attracted to her.

The Center had assured him that they understood the Maltaffian need for some level of bonding before conception could occur during mating. He figured if the match were a nice enough person, he would feel his body become comfortable and ready fairly quickly, within a few days, most likely.

But he was starting to feel as if Alexis had quickened his seed with her very first glance.

Now he was anxious to get her alone and see if he could get her to feel the attraction, too.

Or did she feel it already?

He snuck a glance at her, but she was already looking up at him expectantly, like there was something he was supposed to do or say.

"Mr. Torrn?" Dr. Oppyx said patiently, as if she were repeating herself.

"Sorry," he said. "I was a little distracted. What were you saying?"

"I just wanted to know if you had any questions before getting started on your activities here at the Center," she said with a gentle smile.

Activities...

"Oh, uh, no," he said. "I think I'm good."

Beside him, he could feel Alexis's shoulders shaking with silent laughter.

He glanced down at her to find her blue eyes twinkling up at him, like they shared an inside joke, not like she was laughing *at* him.

"Excellent," Dr. Oppyx said. "Then, without further ado, the two of you may head out. You can use the rear door, through the kitchen."

Alexis wrapped her small hand around his larger one and they headed for the kitchen.

He felt like a little kid again, his best friend dragging him off on daring adventures.

As they passed the counter and sped through the stainless steel of the kitchen, he realized the truth of what this week could be.

If he let go of his deep desire for a child, which was not

really in his control, then what was left of the time here was just having fun - beautiful settings, manufactured adventures, all with a slip of a girl who seemed to have a fire in her.

Whatever happened here, it would be money well spent.

"You're a daydreamer, aren't you?" Alexis asked him as she threw open the back door of the diner.

He winked at her and enjoyed the way her cheeks blushed pink.

She *did* feel the attraction.

Even though they had entered the front of the diner from a summertime beach, they stepped out the back door into an overcast, autumn afternoon. The air was cool with an edge of real cold on the breeze.

Before them ran a stretch of gravel road, with beautiful trees covered in colorful scarlet, yellow and russet leaves on either side.

"Alexis and Tiago," a disembodied voice seemed to say from directly overhead. "I'm delighted to welcome you to your first adventure here at the Center."

"Oberon?" Tiago guessed.

"Correct," Oberon said. "I'll be here throughout your stay to arrange your activities, but also to help with anything you might need. Feel free to call my name at any time and I'll do whatever I can to ensure your stay is a pleasant one."

"Thanks," Tiago said. "Looking forward to it."

"Now," Oberon said. "Your first mission is to get to the farmhouse for dinner."

Right on cue, Tiago's stomach rumbled. His metabolism was so stoked by constant exercise that he was just about always ready to eat. He hoped Alexis hadn't heard.

"You'll have to solve an old-fashioned corn maze to get to the house," Oberon said. "Here comes your ride."

The muted sound of hoofbeats came from just down the gravel street. A huge, dapple-gray creature he didn't quite recognize pulled a cart full of hay.

Was this a joke?

"A hayride," Alexis squealed, her hands clasped together in what looked like rapture. "With a real horse!"

"Is that a Terran thing?" Tiago asked.

"You're going to love it," Alexis assured him. "Come on."

She practically danced up to the beast, and he followed, caught in the undercurrent of her excitement.

"Hello there," she was murmuring gently to the horse.

It lowered its head and made a snuffling sound.

"I'm sorry big guy," she told it. "I don't have a treat for you."

"Check the box on the cart," Oberon's voice suggested.

Alexis's eyebrows went up and Tiago had to chuckle at her as she scrambled for the cart, pulling a small, pale-red apple from the box.

"Here you go," she told the horse, holding it out on her open palm.

Tiago didn't have any experience with Terran horses, or even Maltaffian farm animals, but he didn't think that was a good idea, given the size of the thing's mouth. He was too far away to snatch her hand back in time.

But it politely took the apple with its lips and crunched it up enthusiastically as Alexis smiled and assured it that it was the most beautiful horse that ever lived.

Tiago wasn't sure that was accurate, but he liked her encouraging nature.

He thought to himself that she would make a great mother and then pushed the idea away.

She would actually make the opposite of a good mother,

he reminded himself sternly. He already knew that much about her.

"You have one hour to make it to the farmhouse and solve the labyrinth," Oberon said.

"We'd better get moving," Alexis said, turning to Tiago with a worried expression.

He was pretty sure it didn't matter. What was the Center going to do? Would they starve them to death if they didn't complete their activities?

But he supposed the timeline made it feel more fun.

"Let's do it," he said, heading for the back of the *hayride.*

There weren't stairs of any kind to get up into the cart. It wasn't a problem for Tiago, but Alexis was too small to get on.

"Let me help you up," he offered, extending his hand.

As she took it, he felt a sizzle of energy communicate to him through her impossibly soft skin.

Were Terrans slightly electrified? He was certain he would have remembered learning that in school.

"I'm going to lift you up," he told her. "Don't be scared."

"I'll be fine with it," she told him. "Trust me."

He wrapped his hands around her waist and was surprised to feel her leap as he lifted.

She was light as a feather, and with her jumping, it felt as if he was barely lifting her at all. Her feet went a foot over the bed and he had to actually lower her down.

"Thanks," she said, wading through the pile of straw to get closer to the front, presumably so she could have a good view of the horse.

He leaped up after her, and was surprised to see her lower herself unceremoniously into the prickly stuff.

"It's a bumpy ride," Oberon said warningly.

"I think that means we're supposed to hang onto each

other," she told Tiago, winking. "Oberon knows what he's doing."

He looked at the low rail around the back of the cart and shuddered at the idea of this small, soft woman being thrown over the side.

"Between my legs," he ordered her as he sat near the front of the cart, where he knew she wanted to be.

She scrambled over and sat in front of him, between his legs, as she was told.

Something ancient and masculine deep inside him swelled with pride at this evidence of her submitting to him.

He wrapped his big body around her small one, reveling in the delicate fragrance of her hair and the shiver of electricity he felt once more as they touched. This was not some trick of her Terran physiology. It was something more.

As soon as he had his arms around her, the horse began to plod forward along the path between the trees. A bird cried out, and then a cloud of blue-black ravens lifted from the trees just ahead, forming a triangular curtain above them before disappearing into the sky.

"Oberon, you really know how to set the stage," Alexis said appreciatively.

"Thank you," Oberon replied.

Tiago would have sworn the voice actually sounded gratified. But that wasn't possible. Oberon was an AI, not a person.

The cart went over a big bump and Alexis was tossed more firmly against him, her backside pressing tantalizingly against his groin.

He forgot all about Oberon as he willed himself not to bury his face in her neck and lift his hands from her waist to cup her small breasts.

It was going to be a long ride.

5

ALEXIS

By the time the autumn colors of the forest on both sides of the road gave way to rolling countryside, Alexis was in a haze of pleasure.

Tiago's arms were wrapped around her, his big body pressed to hers, making her feel safe and overstimulated at the same time.

She could sense the tension in him, his muscles tightening each time a bump or curve in the road pressed her closer.

How in the world were they supposed to solve a labyrinth and eat dinner before they gave in to the temptation that hummed in the air between them?

She tried to shake off the feeling. As was the custom on Terra-58, until a woman gave birth to her primary heir and then was matched and married, she did not engage in sexual contact of any kind. Alexis had never been with a man. And she wasn't a believer in instant chemistry anyway. That kind of thing was for the holo-serials her mom watched.

But would it be so bad to lean in? After all, a one-night-stand was exactly what she was here for. Maybe several nights, if she was lucky.

"The farmhouse is up ahead." Oberon's voice interrupted the direction of her thoughts. "You can just see the labyrinth leading up to it."

Sure enough, a lumpy white-stucco farmhouse with green shutters stood silhouetted against the pink sunset atop the hill they were heading for. A golden maze of corn stalks covered the hillside leading up.

Surrounding the farmhouse was a collection of twisted, knobby-limbed trees dotted with red.

"An apple orchard," Alexis exclaimed. "It's like a farmhouse from a storybook."

"A Terran storybook?" Tiago guessed. His deep voice emanated from his chest, and she felt it against her back.

"Yes," she said. "And the diner back there reminded me of a diner I like on Terra-58. Maybe they're trying to help me feel at home?"

He began to chuckle.

"What?" she asked.

"I thought the diner was for me," he said. "My parents run one."

"A Terran-style diner?" she asked, incredulous.

"Your people got one thing right," he said.

"Let me guess, coffee?" she laughed, rolling her eyes, though he couldn't see.

"How did you know?" he asked her.

"Everyone says it," she laughed. "I'm glad our hot bean juice is a hit with other species. But I had no idea old fashioned diner culture was part of it."

"Fried foods and hot coffee are just about universally loved, especially served together," he told her. "Believe me, we had every species you can imagine visit the diner."

"Did you work there too?" she asked.

"When your parents own a diner, you work there," he told her. "I didn't mind though. I learned a lot. And for the most part, the people were nice."

The horse began ambling off the road and onto the grassy area leading up to the maze.

"Once you solve the labyrinth, you'll head up to the house," Oberon said. "There will be a nice meal and some hot apple cider waiting for you."

"Cider," Alexis groaned appreciatively.

"What's the difference between cider and juice?" Tiago asked.

"I'll let Oberon take that question," Alexis said. "I'm a city girl."

"I would be delighted to explain," Oberon said. "But perhaps you'd like to wait until you reach the house? Your time is running short."

"Sure, good thinking," Alexis said. "Ready, Tiago?"

He let go of her and hopped over the side of the cart, then waited below, his arms extended for her.

In the pale pink light of sunset, his russet horns and skin almost glowed with rich color. His massive size and strong arms gave her all the confidence she needed to jump.

He caught her effortlessly, cradling her like a baby against his chest.

He will be an incredible father...

But she wouldn't be around to see it. The thought broke her heart a little.

She wiggled a bit, and he placed her down on the lush grass of the hillside.

"Our staff tried the maze in order to ensure it could be solved," Oberon said. "The fastest time of any two-person team was twenty-eight minutes."

Alexis felt a little sizzle of competitiveness just under her skin.

She scanned the hillside, certain they could beat that time. The maze wasn't *that* big. Before she could begin, movement from somewhere in the maze caught her eye. She tried to focus on it, but couldn't spot anything.

"Oberon," she said. "Are any of the staff in the maze now?"

"No," he replied simply.

A wild idea occurred to her.

"Is there anything *guarding* the labyrinth?" she asked.

"Not currently," Oberon assured her. "Would you like me to add something?"

Not currently?

"No thank you," she told him.

"What made you ask about that?" Tiago asked.

She scanned the hill again, but still didn't see any more movement. Maybe it had just been a trick of the fading light.

"Nothing, really," she told him. "It's just that in the old stories, sometimes there's a minotaur."

"What's a minotaur?"

"A big, strong guy with horns," she explained.

Tiago cleared his throat.

"Yeah," she admitted. "I heard it as soon as I said it."

He chuckled, and she was surprised at how easily her own laugh joined his.

"Are you ready to begin," Oberon asked.

"Let's do this," Tiago said, a pleased and slightly aggressive note in his deep voice.

She smiled, recognizing the tone of a fellow fierce competitor, and took his hand as they marched into the corn.

The air was redolent with the scent of fallen apples,

sweet hay, and molding leaves. With Tiago's big, warm hand around hers, Alexis felt a sense of coziness descend over her, even as they strode quickly down the first corridor.

But when they reached the end, an odd sight awaited.

"We could see this part from the grass, right?" Tiago asked, confirming her suspicions.

"Yes," she said. "It branched into two parts, not three."

"That's what I thought," he said, frowning.

"Should we go back and look?" she asked.

"Let's go right," he suggested. "There should be a single option to turn left."

"I'll wait here," she told him.

His eyebrows went up, but he didn't argue.

She watched him stride down to the righthand path and disappear into the corn stalks.

A raven cried out overhead as it flew for the orchard and a little shiver went down her spine.

"Now there are two possible ways to turn," Tiago said, returning to her. "I think the whole maze is changing around us."

That explained the movement she'd spotted before.

"Let's go out and watch," she suggested. "Maybe there's a pattern to the way it shifts."

She held her breath as they headed back, hoping the maze hadn't changed so much that they couldn't get out again.

But the exit was right where they had left it, thankfully. They stepped out together and looked back up the hillside once they had a couple paces of distance.

They scanned the labyrinth for a few minutes, but nothing appeared to be moving, except the tassels on the cornstalks as the cold breeze moved through them.

"It's definitely shifting," Tiago said finally. "Just not while we're watching."

"I mean the whole place is computer designed," Alexis realized out loud. "I guess it doesn't have to behave consistently."

It was an odd thought. After all, everything looked and felt and smelled so real. But in reality, she might as well be on a giant game board.

"If it changes, how do we deal with that?" Tiago asked, frowning. "If we can't learn from what we already did, does that make it unsolvable?"

"This reminds me of something," Alexis murmured.

"What?" he asked.

She searched her mind for the puzzle piece of familiarity.

"Tech rehearsals," she said, lighting on it.

"What are tech rehearsals?" Tiago asked.

"They're the first rehearsals in the theater," she explained. "Before we have costumes, when we're just figuring out lighting and sets."

"You're an actress?" he asked.

"Ballet dancer," she told him.

"Wow, a ballerina," he breathed. "I should have guessed."

"Technically I'm just a ballet dancer," she said. "Only principal dancers are called ballerinas. I've been a soloist and in the corps de ballet."

"Amazing," he said, looking a little starstruck. "Ballet is really hard."

His attitude endeared him to her. Many athletes didn't think of ballet as anything but a bunch of prancing around in costumes. She wondered if he had known any other dancers.

She did her best not to think about just how many women a guy who looked like him might know.

"I think we need distance," she told him. "Figuring out lighting and scenery placement can't be done from the stage, the guys in the booth have to help the crew get it right."

"But even if we study it from here, when we go back inside again it will just change," Tiago said.

"What if *one* of us goes back out and just yells to the other what to do?" she offered.

"That's a damned good idea," he told her. "Want to go back in there and I can tell you what's going on with the maze?"

"Oberon, do we have to stay together?" she asked.

"You do not," Oberon said.

She swore he was trying not to laugh. But of course, that wasn't possible. Oberon wasn't a sentient being. He was an AI.

"Great," she said. "Let's give it a try, Tiago."

He gave her a wide grin and she dashed off into the maze again.

This time, when she reached the center, she saw three possible turns again.

"Can you see how much it's changed?" she called to him.

"Looks the same to me," he said. "Go right."

She made the first right and saw that there were now three more possible turns, not just the two Tiago had seen before, and three times as many as the one she had seen from the hillside.

"Left," Tiago called out to her.

She turned and saw two more openings, but waited for him to yell to her which way to go.

It was relatively slow going, but Tiago shouted out

instructions with a steady confidence that made her think that he could only see the correct option from his place on the hillside.

By the time she stepped out on the other side of the maze, she had attuned herself to his voice so that she could jog and barely had to slow down before making the turns.

"Yes," she yelled. "Time?"

"Eleven minutes so far," Oberon said instantly.

"So far?" she asked, panting.

"Only one of you is through the maze," he pointed out.

"Right," she said. "Come on, Tiago, I'll guide you."

"Can you even see?" he shouted up.

"I remember," she yelled back.

"Seriously?"

"Come on," she called impatiently. "In and then right."

He wasn't yelling to her anymore, so she figured he was in.

"Next turn is a left," she yelled, hoping the maze would at least hold the shape it had when she was in it. Since she couldn't see what he was up to it didn't seem sporting for it to work otherwise.

A few minutes later, she could hear his footsteps as she called out the turns.

At last, he burst out of the stalks, laughing.

"Yes," she yelled again. "Time?"

"Seventeen minutes," Oberon announced. "A new record."

She pumped her fist and did a little celebration dance.

"How did you do that?" Tiago demanded, running a hand through his long, dark hair.

She shrugged.

"Did you write it down or something?" he asked.

"I've spent my life trying to pick up choreography on the

fly," she said. "I guess I just remember a lot of physical stuff like that."

"Wow," he said.

"But don't ask me to do math in my head or anything," she warned him with a self-deprecating laugh.

"Don't do that," he said, straightening up and fixing her with a very serious look.

"What?" she asked, caught off-guard.

"Don't be modest," he said. "You're super-smart. Own it."

She smiled at him like an idiot, but inside she felt something shift, as if some long held belief about her intelligence were being gently nudged off balance.

"That kind of smarts could save your life one day," he told her. "And it's the same kind of intelligence the explorers used to run the systems before the days of ship-stream navigation."

"Thanks," she said, meeting his eyes without apology.

"Are you ready for dinner?" Oberon asked.

"Yeah, that sounds great," Tiago said, a note of relief in his deep voice.

"Excellent," Oberon said. "Just head right up to the house. The door will open to your palm."

"Thank you," Alexis said.

"It is my pleasure," the AI replied. "You might also like to know that I have relayed your time score to the biological staff. Some are celebrating your prowess, while a few are loudly mourning their own loss. But everyone is impressed."

"Thank you," Tiago said, looking around in the air above his head as if trying to make eye contact with the disembodied voice of the AI.

Alexis found herself smiling at him indulgently for the second time since they met.

6

OBERON

Oberon's drives were humming with excitement.

He began systematically turning off background applications and putting them in stand-by mode to cover up the furious processing he was doing in the foreground.

His subjects were getting along very, very well.

Oberon had been instructed to read thousands of romance novels prior to designing and implementing the Center. In doing so, he had become fascinated with love, and secretly eager to act as a true matchmaker. Instead of just creating an atmosphere that encouraged conception, he quietly tried to encourage love as well.

And he had seen two beautiful successes already. They were a drop in the ocean of clients, but worth his trouble, even if he had to hide his motives from the biological staff.

Since the couples were matched by an off-site program, they were often compatible physically but not emotionally.

However, when Alexis and Tiago's files were uploaded to his system, he had seen with great excitement that they had much in common.

A fighter and an artist might look different on the outside, but they both were perfectionists, each driven to outdo themselves daily in a physical pursuit that was more solo than team oriented.

And he had just seen their competitive natures lock in at the same time in order to make extremely short work of his labyrinth.

He set one background processor to the task of making the activity more difficult for future use. Maybe Alexis had been onto something when she'd suggested a guard?

While that was running, he focused on the results of his scans.

Oberon had been on high alert as he monitored their blood pressure and hormone levels during the activity. He knew they were both in incredible physical shape, so there was no reason jogging through a hillside labyrinth should have skyrocketed their heart rates.

It didn't take him long to conclude that her physical presentation indicated excitement.

Alexis might not know it, but Oberon had analyzed the fights and schedules of four generations of Maltaffian fighters. With seventy-eight percent accuracy, he could state that Tiago Torrn, born Santiago Torres, was the most competitive Maltaffian fighter that had ever lived.

The man fought like his life depended on it. He fought as if he had a huge family of starving children at home, rather than a comfortable mother and father with a thriving small business.

Oberon could not help but run a few simple simulations on what might happen if the biological child of these two beings were to inherit their drive and set its sights on medicine, system-wide peace, or charity. Channeled properly, drive like that could be the heart of a generation.

And there did seem to be an attraction.

It wasn't the agony his last couple had faced trying to keep their hands off each other, so he did not think it was the Maltaffian true mate bond.

Not yet, anyway.

Instead, he read what appeared to be enhanced pleasure readings each time the two touched or their eyes met.

Though the Center's programs didn't track such things, Oberon did. Simple glances and touches were at the heart of a great romance, if all he had read was correct.

As the two stepped into the farmhouse, he searched his back-up for a second evening activity to help them break the ice, since they had arrived so quickly for dinner.

It gave him a response that he catalogued for later exploration, but for now, classified as what he understood to be *fun*.

7

ALEXIS

Alexis watched Tiago open the farmhouse door with a big smile on her face.

It was low-ceilinged and lovely, just like in the storybooks. Tiago had to duck a little to step inside.

Once he cleared the threshold, she could see the wooden floors with rag rugs at intervals, and the fire crackling in the brick fireplace. Lumpy plaster walls and blackened metal knobs and fixtures all fit the theme so perfectly that if she didn't know she was at the Midsummer Center, she would swear she was on Old Earth.

"It smells amazing," Tiago growled, sounding like he was ready to tear the walls down to get to the food.

He stalked through the living room to get to the big kitchen beyond, where a massive, wood-plank table practically groaned under a sumptuous feast.

Alexis felt her tummy rumble, and then an unwelcome thought entered her mind before she could stop it.

Don't go crazy, piglet. You'll never dance again.

She wasn't a pig, of course. She knew she was a healthy

young woman, on the thin side. Eating was essential to maintain her muscles and keep dancing.

Old thought patterns just died hard.

"Outstanding," Tiago breathed, his eyes caressing the meal with a fond carelessness she could only envy. "I'll fix us some hot apple drink."

He turned to the stove, where a pot of steaming cider was simmering, sending up the delicious scent of cinnamon.

She decided to take advantage of him being distracted to do a quick scan of the food for her bracelet.

As she walked closer, she was happily surprised to see that most of what was on the table was vegetables. But they glistened seductively in a way that made her pretty certain they were cooked in obscene amount of butter and cream.

She tapped the bracelet and glanced over at Tiago.

He was rummaging around in the cupboards, most likely looking for mugs.

She scanned the table slowly from one end to the other and waited for an image to pop up with a rundown on each dish and a plan of attack that met her nutritional needs and ensured that she consumed enough calories for the day.

A loud chime dinged on her bracelet.

"Any two green dishes, one white dish and one meat or cheese dish on this table and your choice of one additional white dish, sweet drink, or cup of fruit will complete your daily food scaffold. Congratulations," it chirped at her before she could silence it.

She could feel her face turning red with shame.

"Sorry," she murmured, belatedly sliding her nutrition helper to silent mode.

"Hey, wow, that's awesome. I have that same app," Tiago yelled excitedly, striding over to the table to join her. "I'm a fighter, so I always have to make weight. But I also need a lot of nutrition to keep me going. It's kind of a pain to keep track, but this makes it way easier."

He was already scanning the table, not even looking at her, giving her a chance to recover herself.

Or maybe he didn't even realize she was embarrassed.

But then she watched him surreptitiously slide his helper out of silent mode and she felt a bone-deep sense of acceptance and gratitude.

His bracelet chimed a moment later.

"*Any six green dishes, three white dishes and two meat or cheese dishes on this table and your choice of two additional white dishes, sweet drinks, or cups of fruit will complete your daily food scaffold. Congratulations,*" it announced brightly.

"I kind of need more than you do," he said, looking a little sheepish.

"You're bigger," she said, smiling warmly at him.

"I feel like I could eat all of it," he said shaking his head sadly as he looked down at the table, clearly feeling as if thirteen items wouldn't be enough.

"I'll bet once you get halfway up your scaffold, you'll feel better," she told him encouragingly, remembering the days when she was first recovering from her illness. Her therapist had told her the same thing, and she was right. The shame and pain tended to fade slowly as she fueled her body. At the halfway point of the daily scaffold, she usually felt more in control.

Hopefully, it was also true for someone needing to eat fewer calories than they wanted.

"Let's find out," Tiago said happily.

She dished food onto her plate as he poured them each a hot cider.

But the table was so covered with food there wasn't really room to sit and eat. And there wasn't a dining room.

"Were there cushions by the fireplace?" Tiago asked.

"I think so," she said.

She carried her plate out, and sure enough there were two cushions and a low table by the fire.

Tiago placed their ciders down on the table.

"I'll be right back with my plate," he said. "Go ahead and start, if you're hungry."

She waited for him, glad they had figured out the maze and navigated the even trickier eating situation. It wasn't like they were getting married or anything, but it was good to feel like they could work together.

"This is really nice," he said, carrying his plate out and lowering himself onto the cushion beside hers.

"I guess it's all planned out," she said, feeling shy suddenly.

"Like, to make it more romantic?" he asked.

"Don't you think?" she asked, gesturing to the fire and the food on their plates.

"Yeah, I don't know how they cooked this," Tiago said. "There's no way they used as much butter as it looks like or I wouldn't be able to eat this much of it."

"Is the meal made specially for us, Oberon?" Alexis asked.

"It is, indeed," the AI replied immediately. "Is it to your liking?"

"It's perfect," she told him.

"Thanks, man," Tiago said.

The fire seemed to burn a little brighter for a moment.

"I am delighted that you are satisfied," Oberon said.

"So, you're a ballet dancer," Tiago said, earning points with her by properly remembering her title. "You must always be counting food segments, too."

She bit her lip, not wanting to put a pall on the evening.

"Sorry if that's too personal," Tiago said quickly. "I don't have much of a filter."

"It's fine," she told him. "I didn't answer right away because it's complicated. Yes, I've always had to watch what I eat, but right now I'm using the app to make sure I eat enough."

He nodded and took a bite of Ardoovian peas, as if to show her he was content to listen.

"I injured my ankle a while back," she went on. "And while it was healing, I was worried I wouldn't be able to dance after. Long and short of it is that I ended up trying to lose weight to help the ankle and my career and then I couldn't seem to stop. I messed up everything and it's taken me a long time to get well again."

"That's a risk in my field too, believe it or not," Tiago said. "If you come close but don't make weight you have to forfeit your purse. And if you don't compete as low as you can go, you end up fighting much bigger guys. It's an easy way to end your career. Good friend of mine developed bulimia trying to cut weight. He's recovering now, but it will always impact him. Almost makes you wonder if it's worth being an athlete."

"Oh, it is," Alexis said right away. "At least for me. I'll take the injuries and the food issues and humiliation any day over working in a cubicle."

He grinned at her.

"What?" she asked.

"Nothing," he said. "It's just... that's what I always say."

"Really?" she asked.

He nodded, his dark hair falling over one eye.

She felt a little shiver of something pass between them. It made her warm all over.

They continued their meal in silence. When they had finished, the cider had cooled enough to sip.

She closed her eyes, savoring the rich, sweet flavor.

"So good," he murmured taking a swig.

"This is really cozy," she said. "I grew up in the city. We never spent time in a place like this."

"I grew up in a diner," he said. "We never had *time* to relax like this. But somehow, I feel right at home."

"Me too," she admitted.

His green eyes twinkled in the firelight, and she couldn't help thinking about what they were going to be doing tonight.

She had thought before meeting him that sex with a prospective parent, if necessary, would be something to endure. She had decided she would endeavor to get through it calmly, with as much dignity as possible.

"Alexis, Tiago," Oberon's voice said. "You solved the labyrinth quickly enough that you have time for a second activity tonight. Would you like to hear more about it?"

Tiago gave her a curious look.

Her eyes went to his sensual mouth, against her will.

"I think we're good," he told Oberon slowly. "Ready for bed, Alexis?"

A delicious shiver of awareness went down her spine.

"Yes," she told him, relishing the way his eyes went slightly hazy with want at that single word.

8

TIAGO

Tiago stood and offered Alexis his arm.

She slid her small hand into his and he pulled her up effortlessly. The woman was so featherlight that she seemed to have hollow bones.

Be careful with her. Don't hurt her.

The idea was a little frightening. Tiago had never considered himself to be particularly rough in bed. But Alexis was tiny compared to most Maltaffian women.

And there was something vulnerable about her, that went beyond the eating disorder in her past. She had talked so calmly about a topic that sent one of his best friends to his knees. It was something more than that, some other fragile thing hiding in her eyes.

Whatever it was, he was determined to protect her from it, to offer her whatever comfort she needed to feel safe as long as she was with him.

She stood before him, looking a little uncertain.

"Should we find the bedroom?" he asked her. "We don't have to do anything you're not ready for, but we could stretch out and talk some more."

"That sounds really nice," she said, looking down at her feet.

He felt a pang in his heart, and it scared him.

No, he warned himself. *You can't fall for her. She's not for you. She's the opposite.*

And it was true. On paper, Alexis was everything he didn't want. Her very choice to be here killed any chance that she was the kind of woman he would let into his heart.

But that didn't mean he couldn't be nice to her.

And it didn't mean this couldn't be fun.

He just had to keep his wits about him - protect her body and protect his heart at all times.

But he was a fighter, he had been born to defend.

The bedroom wasn't far. The whole farmhouse seemed to be made up of only three rooms. He opened the door to reveal another cozy fireplace, a view over the apple orchard through two massive windows with a window seat, and a gigantic bed that took up the rest of the space.

"Wow," Alexis said.

"Nice big bed," Tiago agreed appreciatively.

"Do you think that's the bathroom?" she asked, pointing to a door. "I think I'd like a quick shower."

A sizzle of heat went through him at the idea of her naked body under the pounding water.

"Check it out," he said, shrugging.

She wandered over and opened the door.

"It's nice," she said. "I'll be really quick."

"Take your time," he told her.

He looked out the window at the trees as the shower turned on. It was beautiful, but somehow desolate out there. The farmhouse was the same way, lovely character, but no artwork, no personal touch, no warmth. He hadn't noticed it until Alexis was out of the room.

Maybe we're supposed to provide that for each other.

He thought about his past flings, and didn't remember a lot of warmth in either direction.

A lot of the women who wanted to sleep with a fighter wanted bragging rights because of his fame, or maybe an expensive gift, or a chance to land him without a pre-up. And some were just having fun, like he was.

In fairness, he was really only looking for the most beautiful bodies he could find, without a thought in the world as to what kind of people were inside.

Sex had been a means to an end, a transaction, the pleasant scratching of an itch.

And somehow, now that he wanted it to be that and no more, he felt a tenderness for the woman on the other side of the bathroom door.

The door opened before he could explore his feelings further.

"That was amazing," she said, her voice a little breathy.

But he couldn't reply. He was too busy looking at the way her damp hair curled around her elegant neck, as if pointing toward the tantalizing sliver of flesh exposed at the opening of her fluffy robe.

"I, uh, should shower too," he said quickly, brushing past her and closing the bathroom door behind him.

Get it together, Torrn, he coached himself as he stripped in record time. *Just clean yourself up, then go out there and get her pregnant. It's that simple.*

He hurried through his shower, then wrapped a much bigger robe around himself, and returned to find Alexis sitting on the bed, looking out the window, just as he had done.

"You were quicker than I was," she said, smiling.

"I was eager to get back to you," he told her truthfully.

She looked down at her hands in her lap, as if she were nervous.

"Again, we don't have to do anything tonight," he told her gently. "And I know the stakes are high, but remember, this won't really be different from any other time you've done it, right?"

She glanced up at him, her eyes slightly widened with surprise.

"Did I say something wrong?" he asked, going over it in his mind.

"I, um, I know things are different on different planets," she said slowly. "Where I come from, we... don't do this at all until there is a child and a marriage."

"You *what?*" he asked.

Surely, he had heard her wrong. He'd met other Terrans, and while they might not be as relaxed in their sexuality as most races, they weren't *that* prudish.

"Terra-58 is different from the others," she said. "Our whole community was planned, not just the terraforming. We are female-led. This is all part of it."

"But where is the child supposed to come from if there's no sex first?" he demanded, feeling instantly embarrassed. Leave it to him to blurt out something that was probably culturally insensitive.

"We use small fertility clinics and purchased seed," she explained. "That way we know that inheritance will be passed down through the mother's side only. Once a woman has a child, she is eligible to find a partner, marry and have more children, in the way you are thinking."

"You haven't done any of that yet," he realized out loud.

"I have tried to conceive at the clinics," she said, her voice quavering very slightly. "But... I was not favored by Mother Stars with a pregnancy."

"Why not?" he asked, then wished he hadn't.

"They say they don't know," she admitted, twisting her hands a little in her lap. "But I think I do."

He waited, unwilling to ask if she didn't want to answer.

"There's a lot more to it, but it's basically my fault," she said softly. "I danced so much and ate so little. I messed up my cycle, maybe forever."

"I'm sorry," he said. "When they told me I had a match, they explained that my seed should awaken your womb. I didn't really know what that meant."

She looked up at him, her eyes luminous with hope.

"And I don't know if it is true," he admitted. "But the Center seems to know almost everything about stuff like this. I hope for both of us that it works like they say it will."

"Me too," she said, a single tear running down her cheek.

Without thinking, he reached over and wiped it away with his thumb, then left his hand there, cupping her cheek.

She leaned into his hand so slightly that he wasn't sure if he had only imagined it.

"This will be your first time," he heard himself murmur. "We'll have to take it slowly."

"What do we do first?" she asked.

He closed his eyes against a surge of unexpected lust at her innocent question.

"Tiago?" she whispered. "Did I say something wrong?"

"No," he whispered back, opening his eyes. "You've done everything just right. But I would like to kiss you now. Would that be okay?"

She nodded, her eyes on his lips in a way that made him want to rip off her robe and show her how he could use his mouth.

Easy. It's her first time.

He leaned in slowly, giving her time to back away if she was frightened.

But she held perfectly still, waiting for him, as if she were holding her breath.

He brushed his lips across hers lightly once and pulled back.

She smiled and tilted her chin up, as if she wanted more.

He leaned in again, pressing his lips to hers gently but firmly this time.

She froze for an instant, then kissed him back, her soft lips pressing to his in a sweet welcome.

He hummed his approval against her mouth, then ran his tongue along the seam of her lips.

She gasped slightly and he took advantage, sliding his tongue just inside her mouth. She tasted like wild mint and honey.

He could feel her body responding to his invasion, softening as her mouth opened further for him.

He fed on her as gently as he could bear, thumbing her mouth open more.

She was shy at first, then her tongue slid against his until they were dancing together.

When his body began to pound with need, he pulled back slightly.

Alexis's eyes were slightly hazy as she gazed up at him, her lips dark and swollen with his kisses.

"More," she murmured.

He kissed her harder this time, ravishing her mouth, letting go of her cheek to clutch her shoulders.

She submitted to his kiss, following his lead, and sending him too close to the edge.

He tore himself away.

"Lie down," he told her, maybe too forcefully.

She lay back onto the pillows, her hazy, blue eyes still fixed on his.

He crawled up beside her and ran a finger down her neck to where the robe pulled together, hiding her from him.

She bit her lip as they both watched the path of his finger.

"Do you want to keep this on tonight?" he asked, allowing her to answer an easier question than its opposite.

Her eyes met his again and she shook her head.

He tore at the robe as if it had offended him, making short work of the belt and slide.

Alexis gasped and closed her eyes.

He managed to rip his eyes from her tantalizing flesh.

"Are you frightened?" he asked her as gently as he could.

"I... no," she said, opening her eyes again, but not meeting his. "Just worried."

"What is it?" he asked.

"Maybe I'm..."

"Maybe you're what?" he demanded.

"Not what you were hoping for," she whispered miserably.

He didn't know exactly how he could make her understand how wrong she was. But he had an idea where to start.

9

———

ALEXIS

lexis wanted to close her eyes against the echo of her own stupid words.

She had spent a lifetime hearing women say they should be happy in their own bodies, that they should be proud to be themselves. And she believed it.

But Tiago was unspeakably gorgeous. He could have any woman he wanted, and probably had.

Her boyish torso was skinny and toned, with none of the pretty curves or womanly softness men went wild over in the social feeds. And her thighs were thick with muscle and a layer of fat no amount of exercise or dieting had ever made her shed.

With make-up, tights, and tutu, she could be made to look like a beautiful young woman.

But naked, she felt all her stress and pain were evident in her body, which she had used as a tool to her aspirations all her life. To Tiago, it must look wiry, battered, and unlovable. Too small and too large, all at once.

You did not come here to be loved.

Tears prickled her eyes.

"Alexis." Tiago's deep voice cut through her pain. "How can you say such a thing? You are a work of art."

She glanced back up to meet his eyes. His voice was rich with emotion, but he couldn't mean what he said.

"Every single hour you've dedicated is painted here in muscle, bone and bruise," he said. "This is a body that was earned. I could never find that anything but incredibly beautiful. Every single inch."

She closed her eyes and let the tears slide down her cheeks.

She felt him shift on the bed and wondered if she had ruined everything. She'd never had sex before, but she was pretty sure you weren't supposed to lie there crying to start things off.

Then she felt his tongue swipe up her cheek, licking up a tear, and then another.

She smiled and soaked in the sweet gesture as his tongue traced a path to her earlobe.

"So beautiful," he whispered before sucking it into his mouth.

She inhaled and placed her hands on his shoulders, basking in the heat of him, even through the thick robe.

He moved lower, to kiss and nip at the place where her neck met her shoulder.

The sensation sent a shiver through her, and she giggled.

He smiled against her skin and nibbled at her.

When she arched her back for more, he slid down to nuzzle one breast. His hot breath against the sensitive nipple made her cry out.

Tiago growled in response and licked.

A heated zing of electricity flickered through her, and she sank her nails into his shoulders, trying to hold onto reality as her body surged with wanting.

Tiago seemed to lose his mind, one hand clamped down hard on her hip as if to hold her still, the other moved to cup her other breast, his calloused thumb sliding over the nipple, making her whine as he licked and suckled the first again with abandon.

Alexis was desperate, her entire body swirling with need. She felt her hips quivering in his hold as he fed on one breast and then the other, moaning against her as if he were trying to feed a bottomless hunger.

He looked like a god gone mad. Without thinking about it, she slid her hands from his shoulders up to lightly caress his horns.

Tiago went still, as if hypnotized.

She explored the delicious texture, smooth yet ridged, silky but hard as diamonds under her hands.

He moaned lightly.

"Does it hurt?" she asked, pulling her hands away.

"It feels so good," he whispered.

She reached for him again, watching his eyes glaze over as she slowly caressed his horns.

Then he was pulling away, lowering his face to press kisses to her belly, then lower still to nip at her hips and nuzzle her inner thighs.

"Alexis?" he murmured, sliding a hand between her legs and nudging against them, as if to open them.

He could have ripped her apart, but even now, panting with lust, he was giving her choices.

She took in a deep breath and allowed her legs to fall apart for him.

He hummed in satisfaction, his eyes fixed on her sex.

Before she had time to feel too self-conscious, he was pressing his lips to her.

The sensation was incredible.

Before she could even react, he parted her gently with his hands, and running his tongue softly against her opening.

Alexis had figured out how to take the edge off her burgeoning hormones when she was a teenager. But that was a clumsy, furtive thing, over in a minute, with a weak twinge of helpless pleasure immediately overwhelmed by a frigid wave of guilt and embarrassment.

It was not in the same universe as what Tiago was doing right now.

He was lavishing her with his hands and mouth, teasing out every shiver of pleasure, finding the most sensitive places to tease and coax, and abandoning them each time just before she could climax.

Her whole body was tight with need, the pleasure buzzing just under the surface of her skin, desperate for release.

On and on he licked and suckled, nudging a thick finger just inside her to massage a place that made her toes curl.

When her whole body was stretched tight with despair, she began to moan and beg.

"What do you want, sweet girl?" he murmured against her pulsing, hungry sex.

"Please, please, please," she whimpered, not even knowing what she was asking for.

"Oh, I like that," he chuckled.

She wanted to scream, but she went still when she felt him latch onto her stiff little pearl and lash it with his tongue as his finger drew lazy circles inside her.

"*Ohhh,*" she moaned as her whole body fluttered around him.

For an instant, she floated outside herself, then the pleasure crashed into her and her whole body was shot through with ecstasy as she tightened on his finger over and over.

"Again," he commanded, just as her shivers were dissipating.

"I can't," she whimpered, trying to wiggle away from his wicked mouth.

But he held her still, redoubling his efforts.

Suddenly, she was seeing stars as the pleasure impossibly blazed through her again, more acutely this time.

"Tiago," she moaned as she felt herself shatter.

"Good girl," he groaned against her, slowing his movements as she came down.

10

TIAGO

Tiago crawled up beside Alexis and fell back on the bed, panting.

She snuggled against him, and he could feel satisfaction radiating from her, filling him with pride.

His own body felt almost sick with need. He was feverish, desire pounding a thunderous rhythm inside him.

"Tiago," she murmured, rolling over to run her hand down the front of his robe.

Her fingers left a sizzling trail of need, but he grabbed her wrist and pulled her hand away. He had pushed her far enough for her first time being touched.

"Why?" she asked, her sweet voice mournful.

"We've done a lot tonight," he told her. "Don't you think?"

"Not enough," she told him, her eyes solemn. "Not enough to put your baby in me."

Her words lit a fresh fire of need in him.

"We have time," he told her, his jaw stiff with restraint. "We have a week."

"But I want you now," she whispered, fingers toying with his robe again.

The words seared into his mind as her small hands deftly untied the belt and released the slide. She pushed the thick fabric off his chest, and it fell away from his hips, revealing him to her.

He watched her eyes drink him in, tracing down his chest to his abs and then pausing on his cock.

Her mouth fell open slightly and he felt himself pulse in response, his body straining for her.

"It's so big," she murmured.

He wondered if she knew that was what all men longed to hear, or if she spoke in fear. He was big compared to her kind, so big compared to that tiny treasure between her legs.

He watched helplessly as her hand trailed down his chest, drifting over his abs to stroke a single finger down his length.

Then her hair tickled his skin as she gently kissed his chest and belly, as he had done to her.

There was something so sweet in her imitation.

He had been handled by women with so much more experience. But Alexis's sweet exploration was sexier than anything that had come before.

He held his breath as she licked his abs, her hands locking around his hips.

"Alexis, you don't have to," he began.

The words died in his throat as he felt her impossibly sweet, warm lips anoint the tip of him.

Pleasure rushed into his senses, and he felt his whole organ go almost painfully rigid, throbbing against her lips as she kissed down his length and back up again with maddening slowness.

"Alexis," he groaned.

But she was licking him now, swirling her tongue and sucking lightly as she explored him, sending him too close to the edge.

"Stop," he whispered, catching her face in his hands.

"Are you ready now?" she asked.

Her eyes sparkled with excitement, and he almost fell apart just looking at her.

"You can try if you want," he heard himself tell her. "Climb on top of me and see."

She took his hands and straddled his hips. She was tiny, but so flexible.

He gasped when she took him in her hands and slid him against the heaven of her pulsing sex.

She hissed in a breath as the tip of him touched her little gem.

Locking his hands on her hips, he prayed to any power that would listen for the strength not to thrust.

Her hand tightened, holding him in place as she tried to lower herself onto him.

But it was a tight fit, and her thighs were trembling.

He reached up and toyed with her a little, so that she quivered against the tip of him.

"Ohhh," she moaned, working herself against him in despair.

The sight of her, hair tousled, swollen lips, stiff little nipples, was too much for him.

He roared in surrender and flipped them over, so that she was pinned beneath him.

"Alexis, is this really what you want?" he asked her, his voice tight with need.

"Yes," she murmured, gazing up at him with so much trust it nearly gutted him.

He cupped her cheek in one hand and used the other to guide himself firmly against her.

She gasped in a breath.

"This will hurt a little," he warned her. "But then I'll make you feel so good."

She blinked her assent.

Gritting his teeth, he pressed inside her with a single, firm stroke.

Stars burst behind his eyes with the pleasure. He fought it, desperately trying not to spill his seed too soon.

She cried out.

"Alexis?" he whispered, holding himself perfectly still.

Her eyes were wide as she gazed up at him and he was struck all over again at their unusual shade of blue.

He saw the exact moment when her pain melted into pleasure.

"Tiago," she breathed, her eyes closing.

"I'm going to move a little," he warned her. "Tell me if I need to stop."

He dragged himself from her heaven so slowly it almost killed him and then filled her again.

Her eyes flew open, and she smiled at him.

He gave her another long, slow stroke and felt her fingernails dig into his shoulders.

"Alexis," he said, like a prayer.

Then her hands were on his horns again, sliding and caressing, sending waves of pleasure through him.

He slipped a hand between their sweat-slicked bodies and massaged her little gem lightly as he thrust again and again.

She cried out suddenly and he felt her flutter along his cock in her third climax of the night.

It was too much.

He yelled her name and let go, jetting into her again and again, the pleasure splintering him as she clenched around him, moaning out her own ecstasy.

When it was finally done, he collapsed on her and rolled them both over so that she was lying on his chest.

His body still effervescent with echoes of pleasure, he drifted into sleep with a light feeling in his heart. It was like happiness, but brighter.

11

————

ALEXIS

Alexis awoke cocooned in luxurious warmth.

She opened her eyes to realize she was no longer in her solo apartment at the Center.

Instead, she was looking out a gigantic double window at lazy snowflakes falling on an apple orchard.

And Tiago's massive frame was wrapped around hers.

Last night thundered back into her mind and she shivered at the memory, feeling as though all that had happened already hadn't been nearly enough, and she needed him to be constantly taking her.

Another glance out the snowy window told her it was morning and that she'd better shower before the bracelet got impatient about breakfast.

She slipped out of his arms, replacing her body with her pillow when he murmured in complaint.

The wood plank floors were frigid under her feet, and a draft slithered around the ancient looking windowpanes.

Well, it was an ancient farmhouse after all.

Wait. No.

It was a brilliant piece of design, and not one tiny aspect of it was by accident.

If the floor was too cold and the window drafty, it was because Oberon wanted it that way.

And if he wanted it that way, what he *really* wanted was for her to crawl back into bed.

She tip toed quickly to the bathroom and started the shower.

"Oberon," she whispered before brushing her teeth. "I don't want you to reply, or you'll wake him, but I'm pretty sure you can hear me. I have to eat breakfast by a certain time each day or my food scaffold is off. It's part of my recovery. But your plan worked, if I didn't have to eat, I would definitely be back in bed. That was very clever."

She felt a little silly about viewing the AI as a friend who wanted reassurance. But Oberon had been nothing but kind and helpful to her. She would rather err on the side of returning his kindness, even if he couldn't perceive it the way she did.

As she had requested, he didn't respond.

But the lights around the mirror seemed to pulse a little brighter for a moment, then fade back to normal. Almost as if the AI were glowing with pleasure.

She smiled and stepped into the gloriously hot water of the shower. It had probably been a trick of the eyes or the electrical system, but it was nice to think it was *possible* the AI was genuinely pleased with her compliment.

When she was clean, refreshed and dressed in the soft, flowing dress over leggings that had been laid out for her, she padded quietly out of the bathroom and headed down the hall to the kitchen.

At home, she mainly ate protein bars along with fresh

fruit and vegetables. It was easier to monitor exact combinations of fat, protein, and carbs that way.

But poking around the cupboards, she didn't see anything like that. There were fresh croissants on the big table, along with a bowl of fruit. The refrigerator was stocked with milk, eggs, cheese, and fresh veggies.

She was just wondering what to do when she heard someone at the door.

"Hello?" a soft female voice called out.

"Hi," Alexis called back.

A moment later, a small woman in jeans and a pale cream sweater with a lab coat on top walked in. Her jet back hair was in a loose ponytail, and she was smiling at Alexis.

"Hey, I'm Dr. Pan," the woman said warmly. "I'm here for your daily check-up. Do you want to eat your breakfast first?"

"Oh, no, I'm fine," Alexis said. "Let's do the check-up."

She tried to push down on the excitement brewing in her, but it was impossible to stop her heart from racing.

After all that had happened between them last night, she was sure to be pregnant. But was it even possible to know that so soon?

Dr. Pan typed something into her bracelet. A hologram lifted from it as her fingers danced in the air.

"How did you sleep last night?" she asked lightly as she typed and swiped.

"Really well, actually," Alexis realized out loud.

"That's excellent," Dr. Pan said. "And what's taking up your headspace today?"

"Well, I'd be lying if I said I weren't excited for the pregnancy scan," Alexis admitted. "Is it too soon to know?"

"It would be no problem to detect, although very few of

our guests end up conceiving on the first night, especially with Maltaffians needing to make a connection first," Dr. Pan chuckled. "But I'm glad to know you two got started trying. It makes the chance of success during your week much higher."

Alexis smiled back, but she knew better. Maltaffians might need a connection to feel comfortable, but Tiago had seemed *very* comfortable last night. He had even taken the time to make sure her first time was pleasurable.

She felt blood rush to her cheeks and begged herself to think about something else.

"Let's get your vitals first," Dr. Pan suggested.

"Sure," Alexis said.

The other woman lifted her bracelet to Alexis's forehead, and it beeped quietly for a moment.

"Temperature is normal," Dr. Pan said, as the hologram flashed and blinked, like it was recording her notes. "Heart rate is normal, fasting blood sugar is in normal range, blood pressure is normal."

Dr. Pan continued moving her fingers swiftly in the air.

"I'm sorry, Alexis," she said lightly after just a moment. "You're not pregnant at this time. But as I say, a pregnancy at this juncture would be extremely rare. I'm seeing every sign that you're in excellent health. Your chances are good."

Alexis felt her heart breaking and all the air going out of the room.

It was only then that she noticed Tiago standing in the doorway.

"I look forward to many more attempts," he told her with a mischievous grin.

"Are you in any pain right now, Alexis?" Dr. Pan asked her, clearly trying to hide her smile.

"No," Alexis lied.

Her body was fine. But she still had an ache in her heart

at coming up lacking again. Maybe if she hadn't had so many negative pregnancy scans before this one it would be different.

But it wasn't Tiago's fault, or the doctor's. There was no reason to share her pain.

"Enjoy yourself, Alexis," Dr. Pan said, making eye contact with her. "Having fun won't hurt your chances, right?"

Alexis shook her head and allowed a small smile to escape.

"Atta girl," Dr. Pan said, smiling back. "You kids have a fun day. I hear Oberon has big plans for you."

"Thanks again," Alexis said, as Dr. Pan headed back out to the door.

Tiago stepped out of the doorway to give her room and moved toward Alexis.

She seemed to really notice him for the first time, and realized he was shirtless, with a pair of jeans hanging low on his hips. He moved with a sinuous grace that had her heart pounding.

Though they had been incredibly intimate last night, she felt a little shy about putting her hands on him again now, but the temptation was almost irresistible.

"Did you sleep well?" he asked, his voice low and growly.

She nodded.

"Me too," he said. "But now I'm starving. Is there anything good?"

"I looked for protein bars or powders, but there isn't anything like that," she said, shaking her head sadly.

"Are you kidding me?" he asked. "You don't really eat that stuff, do you?"

"You don't?" she asked, stunned.

"I mean not unless I'm on the road or in a pinch," he

said. "They're tasteless and full of chemicals. And crazy expensive. It's much better to cook."

She smiled at the idea that a prize fighter would be worried about the cost of protein bars.

"You can cook?" she asked dubiously.

"Please," he said. "Have a seat. Observe."

She sat and watched as he started a pot of coffee, his muscles bunching and stretching enticingly with every movement.

"That doesn't count," he told her, spinning around. "It's just coffee."

"It counts to me," she laughed. "I use a pod-bot."

The look of horror on his handsome face made her laugh again.

"I'm going to pretend I didn't hear that," he decided, turning back to the refrigerator, and giving her a fantastic view of his broad shoulders and muscular back.

She smiled to herself as he started pulling vegetables and eggs out of the fridge. It was easy to envision lazy, light-filled mornings like this one, relaxing in the kitchen and enjoying breakfast and good company.

It's not real, she reminded herself sternly. *It's not forever.*

But if there was a baby, that would be forever. Tiago would have a daily reminder of her, even if she were worlds away.

Suddenly, she had a vision in her mind of their child, with his green eyes and beautiful golden horns peeking out of dark hair like hers.

Something wrenched inside her, and it was all she could do not to weep.

How could she leave that child behind?

In that moment, success felt like it would be even more painful than failure.

"You okay?" he asked, stepping over to her with a mug of steaming coffee. "You look like you just saw a ghost."

"I'm fine," she managed, taking it. "I guess I'm just a little tired."

"I wore you out, huh?" he asked, quirking an eyebrow.

He was standing so close.

Her body responded instantly, blood rushing to her cheeks, a delicious shiver going down her spine.

"You sure you need breakfast, Alexis?" he murmured, reaching out to stroke her cheek.

A ding sounded from his bracelet, breaking the hum between them.

"The eggs," he said, jogging back around the table to tend to their breakfast.

The scent of the eggs and sizzling vegetables in the pan next to them was incredible. Her stomach rumbled happily, reminding her in uncertain terms that this was much better than a protein bar.

I'll worry about going home later, she told herself. *For now, I'll do what Dr. Pan said and have fun.*

Over at the stove, humming over the eggs, Tiago was gigantic, godlike, and happy as a child.

She smiled indulgently at the big Maltaffian. If he could relax, so could she.

12

———

OBERON

Oberon scanned the readings of Alexis's vitals twice more before backing them up and filing them.

Though of course Dr. Pan was right, and day-one gestations were all but unheard-of for Maltaffian matchings, he was still just a little disappointed at today's result.

The instant connection between the fighter and the dancer had been easily measurable through heart rate, hormone levels and a sense of prediction Oberon had picked up in the last few weeks.

He was certain the *sense* was merely an imperceptible early background data analysis, but he associated it with the biological term *gut instinct.*

Oberon didn't have an actual gut, but he was very sure that if he did, it would have told him immediately that Alexis and Tiago were a perfect match.

It wasn't just their shared interest in physical activities, competitive spirits, or even their similarly humble outlooks, in spite of great success.

Last night, they had neglected to ask Oberon for privacy

mode before beginning their mutual seduction, and he had been able to analyze their effects on each other in great detail.

While he would not share the intimate footage with the biological staff, since nothing violent or dangerous had transpired, he did review it again himself to see if perhaps he had missed some minor hostility that would have prevented bonding.

Different cultures sometimes had nuances that could make a small thing a big issue, especially in such a setting.

But even after scanning several volumes of Maltaffian etiquette, and the only Terran one in existence, he found nothing that could be remotely interpreted as hostile in either of their actions.

As a matter of fact, from all the romance novels he had read, Oberon determined that the couple's activities had been the opposite of hostile, even after multiple viewings.

Tiago had treated Alexis with a respect that looked a lot like tenderness, going slowly when she needed it in spite of a need of his own that read almost like agony on his scans, and then unleashing himself to give her the passion she craved when she was ready.

And Alexis had enjoyed her deflowering, climaxing repeatedly, and encouraging her new lover with lavish praise through her cries.

No, there was something else wrong.

Oberon only wished he knew what.

There had been moments, outside of the bedroom, when each had hormonal readings that showed stress or sadness. But that was natural. No one wound up at the Center without some sadness coming before. And biological beings were not like Oberon. They could not wipe an unhappy memory or overwrite a difficult tangle with a swifter solution path.

Determined to get to the root of their emotions, Oberon shuffled his plan for their day. He scanned his lists, choosing two particular activities that would allow for more shared feeling, and also for more quiet reflection.

If music be the food of love, play on, he recited to himself from one of the great rom-coms of Terran history as he mapped their route between activities, making sure to allow time for healthy eating at each stage.

If Tiago got hungry or Alexis became concerned about her bracelet, he knew any small worries might loom larger in their minds. Biological worries were always just below the surface for biological beings. Oberon had learned this important lesson slowly but thoroughly. Access to robust plumbing and ample nourishment were really the most important features the Center provided. Without those two things, even the most romantic setting or activity in known history wouldn't get them anywhere.

Expanding his scheduler to accommodate changes to their week, he reminded himself that this was truly only their second day at the Center. There was plenty of time for friendship to develop into a bond, and a bond into love.

Perhaps tonight he would review some of his favorite romance novels and scan them for similar situations that might help him set these two on the right path.

Of all the couples who had ever met at the Midsummer Center for Fertility, Oberon suspected these two were among the most likely to fall in love. If they went their separate ways after this week, Oberon felt that it could only be due to something lacking in him and his design.

"Everything okay with the scans, Oberon?" Dr. Pan asked from her office.

He cursed himself inwardly for allowing so much of his memory to be utilized on scheduling. Surely, she would see he was scheming, or think something was wrong and try to reboot him.

"Yes," he told her. "I'm reworking the schedule to allow more time for bonding since last night was more successful than expected by a factor of eight."

"Eight, huh?" Dr. Pan asked thoughtfully. "That must be some footage."

"I cannot share it with you or the other staff unless there is something of concern on it," Oberon reminded her.

"Oh, gods no," Dr. Pan laughed. "I do not want to see it. I would never be able to look them in the eyes again."

"Very well," Oberon said.

Dr. Pan went back to her work, and he scanned his systems and all online references to people *looking into each other's eyes.*

It seemed that Dr. Pan was referring to shame. But did she mean shame for herself or shame for Alexis and Tiago?

And why would any of them be ashamed? They were each doing exactly what they were meant to do at the Center.

It was an interesting puzzle, but Oberon could not spare any part of his memory for untangling it if he wanted to keep working on his matchmaking in the background without drawing more unwanted attention.

13

TIAGO

Tiago had his arm wrapped around Alexis's slim shoulders as the fancy hovercar rushed them past the orchard and back to the winding path that led to the beach where he had entered the Center.

Fields of wildflowers blurred as they traveled, and Alexis let her head fall back as she laughed.

Tiago liked riding in fast cars, too. They had a lot in common.

Not everything, the little voice in the back of his head reminded him. *Not the most important thing.*

He ignored the voice and pressed his lips to the top of the little Terran's head. She smelled like sunlight on a field of flowers.

"Where do you think we're going?" she asked.

"Maybe back to the beach?" he guessed.

"But look how we're dressed," she noted.

He glanced down at his jeans and t-shirt and her cute dress.

"Doesn't seem like we're going swimming," he agreed, frowning.

She laughed again and he smiled down at her, glad she was feeling lighthearted.

He needed to take a page from her book. She was living in the moment, not dreading the end of the week. He should be doing the same.

So serious, his mother would tell him, when she caught him looking out the window, thinking about the past and the future.

He was serious. But was that such a bad thing?

"Here we are," Oberon said.

The hovercar slowed and Tiago found himself staring at a massive beach house above a stretch of frothy water smashing into black lava cliffs.

Though it could only be late morning, a rainstorm made the setting dark as night.

"Whoa," Alexis murmured.

The house itself was a towering oblong rectangle of glass, half-suspended over the side of the cliffs. The warm light pouring from it juxtaposed the cold metal and glass, making it feel more like an ultramodern lighthouse than the setting for a horror holo. Barely.

The hovercar rose to the top of the cliff and then lowered itself onto the gravel parking area. As soon as the doors slid open, they were greeted by the thumping bass of the music inside.

"A party," Alexis said, sounding surprised.

"Something like that," Oberon allowed.

She shrugged and then looked back to Tiago, as if for permission.

He felt that twinge in his chest again, but he simply nodded.

She flew up the stairs to the front door, through the rain

with an effortless grace. He found himself watching instead of following.

"Come on," she said when she reached the top, waving for him to join.

He jogged after her, cool rain pelting him until it dripped from the tips of his hair.

When he reached the top, she placed her palm on the sensor.

The door swung open to reveal a high-ceilinged, open space. The floor looked like marble, but the small tiles were lighting up, seemingly at random, in a rainbow of different colors.

A small crowd of people leaned against the glass walls, holding an array of colorful beverages. Tiago recognized a few of them, and realized they must work for the Center. Were they all taking a morning off to have a party? Maybe it was someone's birthday.

The way they all clung to the walls reminded him of middle-school dance mixers. Since becoming a fighter, he seemed to be surrounded by over-confident people all the time. There was something about these shy wallflowers that made him feel nostalgic.

Once they were all the way inside, the music faded out and the lights came up slightly.

"Welcome to the Dance Games," Oberon announced. "You're going to compete for prizes in a competition that will help you show off your rhythm and moves."

"Oh no," Alexis moaned.

"What?" Tiago said. "You're literally a professional dancer."

"Ballet is a set of very specific positions and movements," she said. "There are endless combinations, but they all come from a single foundation of skills. Free improvisation isn't part of it."

"What are you saying?" he asked, feeling like she was turning a very simple question into a term paper.

"I've never danced in a club," she said simply.

"What?" he repeated, feeling supremely stupid.

"Training for me means getting a lot of sleep and not risking my body on other forms of dance," she told him.

"But you've danced at parties?" he ventured.

"Not really," she said. "A slow dance here and there at a cast party, but I really have only danced formally. I assume you don't fight for fun."

She had a point, although he suspected that dancing at a party would turn out a lot better than punching someone. Maybe she just needed the right partner.

"Well, you're going to love this," he decided, offering her a big smile.

She smiled back at him gamely.

Oberon began to explain the instructions. They were to stay with the rhythm of the music, try to use some of the moves demonstrated on the hologram, and get extra points for hitting the tiles as they lit up.

"When the first one of you reaches one hundred points, it will stop raining and there will be a picnic on the beach for you and all attending staff members," Oberon wrapped up.

So, it wasn't going to be a team activity, then.

The people gathered along the walls cheered and Alexis's eyes lit up.

Mother Stars, but she was competitive. Just like him.

Tiago jogged a little in place, loosening up.

Alexis's eyebrows went up, then she began doing the same, stretching for the floor and brushing her palms flat against it without bending her knees like it was nothing, then stood and lifted her foot over her head.

One of the folks against the wall in a lab coat whistled as if to say *wow*.

Not to be outdone, Tiago threw a few shadow punches, and the room went wild.

He was pleased with himself until he looked over to see that Alexis was doing a handstand, her legs extended into a split. The applause was obviously for her.

"Show off," he whispered.

She grinned at him upside down before flipping back to her feet.

The music started and a holo film began to play, showing dancers moving in a fairly simple way.

Tiago started in, putting his own flair on the moves.

But when he looked up at Alexis, she was simply staring at the moving images.

"Come on," he told her. "It's fun."

She gave him an uncertain smile and then began to move.

Tiago watch in awe.

Alexis was an undeniably beautiful Terran. She was graceful, strong, and nicely dressed. And she was copying the movements of the dancers on the hologram almost precisely.

But somehow, everything about it was wrong.

It was like he had gone to a Vystian rock concert and was watching the Upper Arkadian Philharmonic Orchestra perform all the songs.

Alexis was hitting all the notes, but it was a recital instead of a rebellion.

"What?" she asked, noticing him looking over.

"It's just... I've never seen anyone dance like that," he said.

"Why did I not get a point for that?" she asked, frowning at the lit floor tile she had just touched.

"Relax a little," he suggested.

"What are you talking about?" she asked him.

"When you dance, it's all about following the rules, isn't it?" he asked her.

She nodded.

"This kind of dancing isn't about that at all," he said.

"What's it about?" she asked.

"I'm not a hundred percent sure," he admitted. "I just know there's a feeling to it - a feeling of being relaxed and having fun."

"I'm having fun," she said defensively.

He managed not to chuckle.

"Come here," he told her. "I'll help you."

"We're competing," she said suspiciously.

"It's not a fair fight if we don't both know the rules," he told her.

She moved toward him, and he was mesmerized by the sensuality of her movement. When she wasn't thinking about dancing, she was so incredibly sexy.

"Now what?" she asked when she stood in front of him, inches away.

"Put your hands on me," he told her. "One on my chest, one on my hip."

She tentatively placed her hands where he said.

Her open palm was warm against his chest. And something about her hand clenching his hip had him envisioning so many things he would like to do to her.

He placed his hands over hers and began to move gently to the music.

"See how the rhythm dictates my movement?" he asked her.

"Your hips are moving around a lot," she noticed.

"That's the idea," he told her.

She laughed.

"What?" he asked.

"Oh, it's just that in ballet, keeping your hips level is kind of the name of the game," she told him. "That and pointing your feet. If my old ballet teacher ever saw me moving like that, her head would explode."

"Well then it's a good thing she's not here," he told her. "Just forget about those rules."

"Easy for you to say," she laughed. "But I'll try."

He held her hands right where they were and watched her start to move with him.

At first, she was as stiff as before. But after a few minutes, she relaxed and started to really move.

"That's it," he murmured encouragingly. "Now get your feet in a wider stance so you can move more."

She moved her feet apart and started up again, dropping her core a little more and working with the music, stretching and contracting with the rhythm as if she were controlling the music, not the other way around.

"That's really nice," he told her, lust starting to simmer as he watched her move.

She winked at him, gave an extra shimmy, then giggled.

A warm sense of happiness washed over him.

This is temporary, he reminded himself. *Don't get attached.*

But it didn't matter. He felt like himself when he was with Alexis, only better, more patient. Ironically, his strait-laced little rule follower seemed to make him more fun.

He let go of her hands, and she began doing all the

moves on the hologram again, only now she was into it, nailing it like she belonged onstage with a band.

Her hips sank and rose, swaying as she tossed her hair and flung her arms toward the stars, an expression of pure joy on her soft, sweet face. She was inhabiting the music, allowing it to move through her.

Tiago forgot to dance. And when the hologram exploded into light, signifying that Alexis had hit one hundred points, he didn't mind a bit.

Even his competitive nature had been tamed by the sweet little Terran.

She turned to him, smiling hard, her eyes luminous with pride.

Tiago felt like he had been living his life in total darkness and someone had finally shone a light on him.

14

ALEXIS

An hour later, Alexis sat on a soft blanket on the beach, looking out over the ocean.

Just as Oberon had promised, the storm had moved on. The sky was a brilliant blue, and the cerulean water glistened all the way to the horizon.

The rush of the waves merrily crashing into the lava cliffs and the happy chatter of the Center staff made a lovely backdrop.

On the blanket beside her, Tiago was demolishing his lunch, eating as much fruit in a sitting as she would in a week.

"Sorry," he said suddenly, his mouth full. "I'm used to eating alone."

"That's okay," she told him. "It makes the meal more fun when you eat it with such gusto."

She didn't tell him that it also made it easier for her to eat her modest portions when she saw his.

"You were incredible today," he told her for about the tenth time.

"It was really fun," she said. "I was surprised. I didn't think I could be good at that kind of dancing. Not that I am - just, you know, I did it. That's all. And it was fun."

"I'm so glad you did," he said.

"You're a really good teacher," she told him. "You're going to make a great dad."

She almost hadn't said that last part. But he was going to make a great dad. She was counting on it, or she wouldn't be able to go through with any of this.

"Thanks," he said, his voice suddenly deep with emotion.

"Do you have a lot of family around?" she asked suddenly. "You know, to help out?"

"My parents stay pretty busy with the diner," he told her. "And I was an only child, so there won't be any aunts and uncles. I'm planning to hire a live-in nanny."

She willed herself not to overthink that. A nanny was a luxury few could afford. Any child would be lucky to have a loving, successful father and a full-time nanny attending to their needs when he worked.

"You were an only child?" she asked, latching onto the other thing he had said.

"My parents weren't able to conceive," he said, shrugging. "I was adopted. But Maltaffian adoptions are expensive and complicated. They like to say I was enough."

He was smiling fondly, and she smiled back, glad he had a loving relationship with his parents and that they had been open with him about his origins.

"Did you ever get to know your birth family?" she asked.

"My birth mother left me on the doorstep of the local Intergalactic Council when I was just a few days old," he said, his smile fading. "When I was a teenager, I told my mom I wanted to find her, and she helped me."

"Wow," Alexis said. "She sounds like an amazing mom."

"She's the best," he said. "Anyway, my birth mother had gotten married a year or so after she had me. She had two other kids, not so much younger than me, and she seemed happy and comfortable."

"How did that make you feel?" Alexis asked carefully.

"Conflicted," he chuckled. "I had imagined her alone and destitute, missing me, wondering about the life she left behind. I thought I would be comforting her. Instead, it felt like she had given me away so she could get to the life she wanted. And she had no regrets."

That was the way these things were supposed to work, as far as Alexis understood it. His mother had surrendered him so that she could provide better for the family she would eventually have. But it still hurt him, and she understood his pain. No one wanted to feel disposable, even if they had ended up in a loving home.

"But I realized that I was happy for her," he went on. "It was really cool of her to let me into her life. Cool of her husband, too. And I liked the idea of having siblings, even if we barely knew each other. We only got together the one time, but we sent Hearth Day cards for a few years afterwards. It was kind of nice."

"I'm amazed that you were able to deal with those feelings at such a young age," Alexis told him.

"A couple of years later, when I started becoming successful in my fighting career, things changed," he went on, his voice turning dry and bitter. "At first, it was just one of her kids, then the other, asking me for money. I wasn't sure how to react. Then it was her too. I had seen for myself how they lived, and they were fine for money, better off than my parents."

"Wow," Alexis breathed.

"When I won my first championship, they filed for the courts to recognize the familial bond, so they could have the rights to inheritance," he said, pain evident in his voice. "And according to Maltaffian law, they now have a direct line to my estate."

Was this the only reason he wanted a child? To block his birth family from his assets when he died? She felt cold all over.

"I know what you're thinking," he told her. "But no, inheritance laws are definitely not the only reason I want a baby. I want a family of my own. And since I haven't been blessed with a mate bond yet, I'd rather do it alone than initiate a marriage contract that could fall apart if either of us finds our mate."

"A mate bond?" she echoed curiously.

"Every Maltaffian has the capacity to form a mate bond," he told her. "It's what Terrans might call a *soul mate,* but it's more than that. More real. There's a physical component that's basically undeniable. Many Maltaffians never find a true mate. But those who do are helpless to resist, even if they are already in a marriage contract with another."

"Oh," she said, thinking about the impossible choice he had in front of him. Would it be better to remain alone than risk destroying a family?

"But don't worry, Alexis," he told her, his green eyes serious. "I will love this baby enough for two. And I would never, *ever* bring a child into the world and then turn my back on it, like my mother did."

Like I will, she couldn't help but think with a pang of pain. *Does he think I want to do that? Does he think I would if I had the choice to stay?*

She searched her heart for the words to tell him how

desperately she wanted to be a mother, how bottomless the ocean of pain would be when she had to walk away.

"It's time to begin your next activity," Oberon said, breaking the silence between them before she had a chance. "Does either of you know how to ride on horseback?"

15

TIAGO

Tiago eyed the massive beast suspiciously.

It stomped one mighty hoof and tossed its midnight black mane, looking like it couldn't decide whether to charge him or eat him. He didn't have much experience with riding a mount of any kind, and he'd never met a Terran horse before coming to the Center. But he was pretty sure this one didn't like him.

"He's so beautiful, Tiago," Alexis murmured.

"I like yours better," he said, glancing over at her stout brown mare with the inky black mane and legs that waited for her patiently.

"She's lovely, too," Alexis agreed, her voice dreamy.

"The two of you will be riding the trail up to the hot springs and the cabin where you'll spend the night," Oberon said.

"Are you sure this thing can handle my weight?" Tiago asked.

The horse was very large, but so was he. The idea of hurting it did not sit well with him. He might not want to be its best friend, but he didn't want to strain its back.

"Everything at the Midsummer Center was either designed or acquired specifically to fit your needs," Oberon reminded him.

"Wait," Tiago said, scrutinizing the creature in front of him, "are you telling me that this horse—"

"—No," Alexis said firmly. "If they aren't real, I don't want to know."

She was scratching the mare behind the ear as it snuffled her chest. Clearly, this was her favorite activity so far.

He cracked a smile in spite of himself.

"Do you know how to mount?" Oberon asked.

"I'll show him," Alexis offered. "We have mounts back home. Nothing like this, of course, but I think it will be the same process."

"Very well," Oberon said. "The process is indeed the same."

"It's easy," Alexis said to Tiago. "I promise."

And just like that, he was lost in her sparkling blue eyes, not caring if he was thrown from the wild beast or any other calamity that might follow, so long as she kept coming closer.

"You always approach and mount the horse from the left," she told him.

"Why?" he asked.

"I'm not really sure," she told him. "I think it had something to do with soldiers and swords in the beginning. Now it's just tradition and the way the horse was trained."

Swords?

"So, you'll approach with confidence, put your left hand on his withers, and your left foot in the stirrup," she said.

"His withers?" he echoed.

"The place where his neck meets his back," she said. "Then swing your right leg up and over."

"That sounds easy enough," he said, nodding. It did not sound easy, but he didn't want to let her see his fear.

"Watch me first?" she offered.

"Sure," he said.

She approached her horse slowly and calmly, even though he knew she was excited.

Just as she described, she placed one hand where the horse's neck met its back, her left foot in the stirrup and swung her other leg over, mounting the animal in a single, fluid movement.

"Ready to try?" she asked him as she reached down to scratch the mare's neck.

"Yes," he said with more enthusiasm. She made it look fun. Maybe it wouldn't be so bad after all.

"Approach him calmly and with confidence," she reminded him.

He made eye contact with his horse.

It snorted at him and stamped a hoof.

"Talk to him gently, in a low voice," Alexis suggested.

"Hey buddy," Tiago said as calmly as he could.

The horse quieted a little, but swished its tail as if it didn't like being condescended to.

Tiago could hardly blame it.

He slowly approached and put one hand on the *withers*.

The stallion's skin twitched under his hand, and it gave its head a shake, like it didn't want to be touched.

"He's just a little grumpy," Alexis laughed. "He'll feel better when we get moving."

Tiago nodded and slipped his left foot into the stirrup. It wasn't as easy as Alexis had made it look. He had to balance, and the angle was odd.

No sooner was his foot in the stirrup than the damned

beast danced his back legs away, leaving Tiago to chase after him.

"Talk to him," Alexis reminded him gently.

"Hold still," Tiago said in a deep, calm voice. "We're going for a walk."

The animal snorted, but mercifully stayed put.

Tiago hopped closer and then swung himself up.

Looking around, he realized he was up pretty high, and the horse was nudging his front leg, leaving Tiago suspended with nothing keeping him on the horse but his feet in the stirrups.

"Excellent," Alexis said. "How do you feel?"

He shrugged, not wanting to seem cowardly. Balance had never been his strong suit. But he was clearly going to need it.

"Next thing to do is get a better grip on the reins," she said. "Look."

He managed to wrest his slack reins up into a fair imitation of hers.

"Now put your heels down and keep them down," she said.

He obeyed.

"Put them down," she repeated.

"They are down," he said, looking at his feet.

They weren't, not really. Not like hers.

"At first it feels like a stretch," she said. "But you'll get the hang of it. Ready to go?"

He nodded helplessly.

"Okay, you're going to squeeze his belly with your knees," she said. "That tells him it's time to go."

He watched as she gave her horse an imperceptible squeeze and it circled around and headed for the trail.

He squeezed his horse gently.

Nothing.

He tried again, a little more firmly.

It lifted its head and snuffled a little, as if to remark that there was absolutely nothing going on.

"Is he ignoring me?" Tiago asked, hoping he didn't sound as whiny as he felt.

"Maybe," Alexis said with just the smallest smile. "He can tell you're an inexperienced rider. Give him a hard squeeze and make a clucking sound when my mare starts walking. He'll follow."

Tiago sighed and waited for her to start moving.

Sure enough, when he squeezed and clucked, the stallion began to plod along after Alexis.

"You're good at this," he told her when they caught up.

"I like animals," she said, shrugging.

But her cheeks were a little pink, as if his compliment pleased her.

He smiled down at her, glad the path had been cut wide enough for them to travel side by side.

"This is actually really nice," he said, meaning it.

"I've always loved the way the woods smell," Alexis said. "It's so relaxing to breathe that fresh air."

"You said you were a city girl?" he remembered.

"The city is fun," she told him. "I love my apartment and the hush rail, and of course we have the big city park. But you're never really alone, you know?"

"Not a lot of solitude in the city," he agreed.

"I like the country," she told him. "I always figured I'd settle down further out when my career was over."

He nodded appreciatively. "Me too."

"Really?" she asked.

"Sure," he said. "I'm tired of living in hotel rooms and buses. Not that I want my career to end anytime soon, but eventually it will. No one fights forever. It's good to have a plan, something to look forward to."

She nodded and bit her lip.

"What are you thinking about?" he asked. "Your country estate?"

"I don't know how much you think ballet dancers make," she laughed. "But rural shack is more like it."

He nodded but didn't speak, wondering if she was going to tell him what had made her bite that pretty lip. And not wondering if she might let him bite it just like that.

"I always imagined myself with a lot of children," she said softly, her eyes on the trail ahead. "That's probably not likely though."

"Why not?" he asked.

"Well, you know I'm here because I couldn't conceive," she said, shrugging. "And even after last night - nothing."

"That had nothing to do with you," he told her, an unfamiliar cold feeling twisting in his chest. "That's only because of me, my seed will be vitalized as we get to know each other."

"It wasn't your fault when I failed at the clinic," she said softly.

"My seed will bring your womb to life," he said, repeating what the Center had told him.

"That's why I agreed to do this," she said, then buttoned her lips.

There was something more she was feeling, something she didn't want to say.

Was she sorry she had come? Did she regret having her first sexual encounter with him?

Last night had been magical, as far as Tiago was concerned - intense enough to make him question how he was going to let her go when this was over. And it was far from his first encounter. Had she not enjoyed it as much as he had?

Before he could answer, the stallion whipped his head to the right so fast that Tiago nearly fell off.

"What in the stars—" he began.

But the inky black horse had taken an enormous bite of red berries from a bush beside the trail.

"Oh, wild raspberries," Alexis laughed. "You can hardly blame him."

"Nah, I get it, bud," he said fondly to the horse. "I get hungry when I'm working out, too."

He watched the animal tear and crunch at the delicate berries with gusto. Normally Tiago was so invested in thundering down the path toward a goal. It was bizarre, and kind of awesome, to let himself get sidetracked for a change.

As if he had heard his rider's thoughts, the midnight stallion suddenly forgot his berries and lunged into the field beyond, leaping a fallen log and sending Tiago up in the air before landing hard again on his back.

"Hey," Tiago yelled. He'd been so interested in getting the beast moving that he hadn't asked any questions about how to stop it.

While up in the air, Tiago had let the reins go slack and now he was having trouble gathering them, as the animal ran faster and faster, banging Tiago around like an egg being scrambled in its shell.

"Just concentrate on staying on," Alexis yelled from close behind. "He'll get where he's going or get tired eventually."

She was following them. She really was a plucky girl. He tried to distract himself with that, instead of imagining what would happen if he flew off into a tree or rock.

"Lean down close to his neck," she yelled. "Try to put

your weight there and on the stirrups, so you can lift your seat slightly."

"My seat?"

"Your, um, your bottom," she yelled. "Try to keep it up, off the saddle, so you don't get banged around so much."

He did as she said, leaning forward and letting more weight rest on the horse's withers and his stirrups. The moment he lifted his ass slightly from the saddle, he felt worlds better. His balance was better now too since he had lowered his center of gravity.

He was still trying to hang on with all his concentration, but he would definitely thank her if the cursed creature ever stopped.

A lifetime later, or perhaps only a few minutes, the rhythm of the stallion's movements finally slowed.

He lifted his head slightly to look around and realized they were approaching a clearing.

The pretty meadow was split in two by a sparkling creek that glittered as the water danced by, around a curve and back into the trees, a mist hovering directly above its surface.

A wooden footbridge connected the two sides. On the far side of the meadow stood a small log cabin with smoke issuing from its chimney.

"We made it," Alexis panted.

He could hear the smile in her voice, but didn't quite dare turn around.

The stallion slowed even more. Its hoofs clattered over the bridge, and it finally came to a stop on the other side, where a large trough of water and another with oats and fruit awaited.

"So those berries were just an appetizer," Tiago said, rolling his eyes.

"Let's dismount and walk him for a few minutes," Alexis suggested. "They shouldn't eat or drink right away after that run."

"Hear that?" Tiago asked the horse as he gingerly got down. "Your plan for an early dinner got away from you."

The stallion snorted and tossed his mane.

Alexis laughed and Tiago laughed too, glad they had made it safely, and glad they had each other's company, even if it was only for a few more days.

16

ALEXIS

An hour later, Alexis eyed the creek. After they had cooled down the horses and eaten a light supper, it was finally time to enjoy the hot springs.

But were they supposed to wear bathing suits or just... get in?

In spite of everything that had happened last night, she was feeling shy all over again about her tiny breasts and big thighs. Would it always be like this? Every single time she wanted intimacy with a partner, would she have to be half mad with desire before she could stop fretting about her body?

She looked up to see Tiago blithely tearing his clothes off.

"What?" he asked, standing on one leg while he peeled his pants off the other.

Before she could answer, he started to wobble.

She giggled as he raced against time to get his pants off and then staggered forward, just saving himself from face planting.

His massive body with its ruby-hued skin looked absolutely perfect in every way. No wonder he wasn't shy about revealing it.

While she stared, he ran a hand thorough his long hair, revealing more of his beautiful horns, which gleamed in the twilight.

Mother Stars, but he was an incredibly gorgeous man.

"Come on," he said, tilting his chin up to indicate the creek. "Let's see if those hot springs are as hot as they say."

She smiled, but somehow couldn't move.

Then he was striding toward her, a sexy smile on his face.

"You're too tired to strip down, aren't you?" he asked teasingly. "Want me to help?"

She nodded slowly, sparks of desire lighting up her blood already.

He smiled and reached for her, and she closed her eyes. If she didn't look, she couldn't see herself. And if she couldn't see herself, she couldn't start a downward spiral.

His hands sent delicious shivers down her spine as he slowly and carefully released her slides, and removed every stitch of her clothing.

At last, she felt the final piece hit the ground at her feet, and the cool, crisp air on every inch of her skin.

"Mmm," he groaned approvingly. "Perfect. Let's go get wet."

She opened her eyes to see that his were hungrily roving over her whole body.

There was not one part of her he didn't view with desire. It made her heart pound.

"Race you to the water," she said, laughter bubbling in her chest.

"Why, you little..." he began as she darted away from him.

She reached the creek and used a set of shallow stone steps cut into the bank to get to the water.

The steam lifting off the surface was deliciously warm. She dipped in a toe experimentally and then moaned with pleasure.

Wading out into deeper water, she found a place where the creek widened. In the center, large, smooth rocks sat at the perfect height for lounging.

"*Mother Stars*," Tiago groaned in pleasure as he waded in after her. "I wish I had this back home."

She settled onto a rock and watched his muscles ripple as he approached.

His green eyes flashed with lust as they met hers.

She gasped slightly, though of course she had known what would happen here - what would happen every night they spent together.

"Are you surprised that I want you?" he asked her.

She shook her head.

"Then what was that?"

He was towering over her now, every part of him focused on her.

"I... I just thought you might be sore from earlier," she murmured stupidly.

"Wild horses couldn't drag me from your bed," he growled.

She smiled.

"That was a poor choice of words," he admitted. "But I didn't come here to play word games, Alexis Clare. I came here to have my way with you. Are you ready for that?"

Every cell in her body shivered with lust.

"Don't you want to relax in the water?" she teased lightly.

"We can do that between rounds," he growled, lowering himself onto her rock and grabbing her shoulders.

"Rounds," she echoed.

His hard body felt incredible against hers under the heated water. She moved against him instinctively, all her fears and worries forgotten.

Tiago cupped her cheek in a big hand and tilted her face up so that her eyes met his.

He leaned in so slowly to kiss her that she thought she would combust.

Then they were feeding frantically at each other's mouths while his cock found her needy sex and he entered her with a long, firm thrust.

She expected pain, but there was none this time, only the insistent ache of desire, pulsing and dragging at her, making her desperate for release.

She tried to jog her hips up, but he pinned her to the rock.

"Nice and slow, princess," he murmured, pulling slightly away from her mouth. "Let's make this first one last."

17

———

TIAGO

Tiago cradled his tiny Terran to his chest, touched that she had fallen blissfully to sleep in his arms even outdoors in the middle of a hot spring.

She trusted him so completely that it almost hurt.

After taking the edge off with one lovemaking session, they had relaxed in the hot water and then ended up all over each other two more times.

Hope flickered in his heart that she might soon be carrying his child.

She murmured something senseless and then snuggled back into him as he lifted her from the water and carried her up the stone steps toward the cabin.

The cool breeze was bracing against his bare, wet skin. He knew she was more susceptible to the elements than he was, so he hurried for the cabin.

His heart throbbed strangely in his chest, and he knew this emotion was not about some unknown child.

It was Alexis he cared for, Alexis he longed to protect. It was Alexis he could not imagine living without.

But how could he love a woman who was willing to have a baby and walk away?

Her intentions in being here at the Center were everything he hated, everything he mistrusted.

She might seem kindhearted and fun-loving. But at the end of the day, she was willing to trade her own baby for a chance at having another on her terms, with another man.

It was exactly what his birth mother had done, and look what kind of person she had turned out to be. She and her new kids were the reason he had felt rushed to take this step in the first place, instead of spending a few more years seeking his true mate.

And now he was tempted to commit himself to someone just like her?

She's not just like her.

But the differences weren't what mattered. What mattered was what a person would do when faced with the most important things in life - their children and family.

He let himself take just a sip of her scent. The fruity, floral sweetness of her hair sank into his senses, half-hypnotizing him.

Enjoy it now. When your time here is over, this is over too.

He opened the door to the cabin. The inside was pleasantly warm from a crackling fire.

The whole space was one big room, with a bathroom walled off in the corner. Colorful curtains and throw rugs in muted tones set a playful mood. A small stove and ice box and a single plank of wood across a metal rack made up the kitchen.

Dried flowers and vegetables hung from the ceiling at intervals. The chairs held stacks of quilts and pillows, as if the whole place were meant to be fragrant and restful.

Large windows would reveal the meadow, woods, and

creek tomorrow. For now, it was full darkness outside, and the interior of the little cabin was all he could see.

A huge mattress had been made up on the floor in front of the fire and he carried her to it, wrapping a sheet around their wet, naked bodies as he lowered them down.

She stirred in his arms, her hands sliding over him, a tiny, needy sound coming from her lips.

She was still asleep, but she wanted him, even as she dreamed.

He felt a tug on his heart that he knew he had to ignore. But her pull on his body was easier to surrender to.

Their time together felt shorter now, so he nuzzled her back, ready to take her again if she woke up wanting him.

He drifted off, thinking about the irony of his situation.

If she wasn't willing to do the unthinkable, she wouldn't even be here. He wouldn't have gotten the chance to meet her, or the chance to have a child of his own.

Alexis was exactly what he needed her to be, which made her everything he could never have.

18

TIAGO

Tiago awoke feeling more at peace than he had been since he was a child.

Alexis was wrapped in his arms, still asleep. Her small form felt just right against his.

He closed his eyes, soaking in the feeling of utter calm.

But it was too late. He was awake now, and a million things jockeyed for position in his brain. Of course, one in particular pushed its way to the front.

Surely, after last night's activities, Alexis was expecting by now. He slid his hand down slightly to cup her abdomen.

Are you in there, little one? I can't wait to meet you...

He was being silly. He should wait to have it confirmed before getting sappy.

But in a part of his mind that he couldn't seem to control, he was already thinking about names and tiny clothes and diapers and cribs and college savings.

He opened his eyes fully and realized the fire from last night was still burning. It must be one of Oberon's creations, since a real fire could not have burned so long without more fuel.

It was incredibly convincing. Even the creosote scent was so real.

He very gently extricated himself from Alexis and found some sweats from the dresser in the room, then hit the bathroom and dressed quickly, hoping she slept a little longer. It couldn't hurt for him to take a quick run before their day got underway, since he wasn't getting his usual workouts.

He turned to check on her before pushing the door open, but she hadn't moved a muscle since he'd gotten out of bed.

Outside, the air was cool and crisp like last night, and the sky still mostly dark. He decided to run around the meadow a couple of times so Alexis wouldn't worry if she woke up before he came back.

The fresh air felt good in his lungs, and though his muscles were still sore from his adventure on the stallion yesterday, they were sore from more fun things, too.

And besides, it was worth being kidnapped by an ill-mannered animal if it made Alexis laugh so hard.

As he took his second lap, he wondered if there were supplies in the kitchen like in the house where they slept the first night. He was eager to show off his cooking skills for her again. It had been a joy to watch her eat with such pleasure.

He knew she had been recovered for a long time, but he could also see how conflicted she felt about her body.

He understood all too well. While he might have women throwing themselves at him after every fight because of his *killer bod,* the truth of the matter was that he was in a constant battle with it, too.

Strength, flexibility, and holding a weight class - each facet came at a cost to the other two. Gaining bulk meant less flexibility and pushing to make weight. Losing weight meant the loss of muscle and held his energy down when he most needed extra workouts and flexibility training.

The whole thing was a precarious balance on which his career rested heavily. And as he got older and bad joints and torn ligaments entered the fray... well he couldn't fight forever. No one could.

The key was to set aside a good nest egg and be realistic about when to quit, so you could do it with dignity. There was nothing worse than seeing an old, punch-drunk fighter bagging groceries on the gossip feeds. Tiago had no interest in repeated concussions or hustling for more credits when it was finally over.

He had a healthy amount of savings now, and hoped one day to have enough to buy some farmland and tinker with growing food and tending to animals if he felt like it, or hiring others to help in case he didn't.

A happy image flashed through his mind before he could stop it. Alexis in a red dress with a white apron, standing in a country kitchen that smelled of gingerbread, twirling around with a toddler girl in her arms and bigger kids around her skirts, all smiling up at her.

That's not what she wants, he reminded himself. *She came here to have a baby for me and go. That's all.*

But the vision had felt so real, like a memory that just hadn't happened yet.

He focused on his breathing and trying to regulate his oxygen intake for the next couple of laps. It was a sufficient distraction, and he finished his run without another unpleasant or overly pleasant thought.

Sliding the door open quietly, he was relieved to find Alexis still sleeping. He had worked up quite a sweat, and he was glad for a chance to shower before she saw him.

He grabbed more clothes and headed back to the bathroom to wash up.

Half an hour later, he was puttering around the kitchen, trying to decide whether to make a vegetable scramble with buckwheat johnny cakes or a plain omelet with a massive fruit salad. Both options were similar in terms of nutritional content, and he could adjust calorie intake to suit them both with portion sizes. Also, and most importantly as far as he was concerned, they were both delicious.

A knock at the door interrupted his decision making.

He strode to open it a crack and was greeted by the sight of the little doctor who had been at the house yesterday morning, standing on the steps, smiling up at him.

"I'm just here for her morning check-up," she said brightly.

"She's not up yet," he whispered. "Should I wake her?"

"According to her vitals she's been awake for three minutes," Dr. Pan informed him.

He turned around and sure enough, Alexis was sitting up with a quilt wrapped around her.

"Sorry, I wake up slowly," she told Tiago with a little smile.

His heart pulsed and he smiled back at her helplessly.

"Is it okay for me to get cleaned up and dressed first?" she asked Dr. Pan apologetically.

"Of course," Dr. Pan said. "Take your time. Maybe we'll make some coffee."

"Perfect," Alexis moaned appreciatively.

Tiago led Dr. Pan up to the counter while Alexis scampered off to the bathroom, a wad of clothing in her hand.

"Seems like you two are getting along well," Dr. Pan said lightly.

Tiago nodded, unable to figure out what to say in return.

I'm falling hard for her.

And the idea makes me sick.

He poured some water into the coffee cell, frowning at it like it had done him wrong.

"How are you holding up after the horse... incident?" she asked as he measured out the coffee. "I can take a look if you have worse than some bruising, or give you a little anti-inflammatory?"

"I'm fine," he told her. "I went for a run already this morning."

"I know," she said with a smile. "The staff was very impressed. Do you need access to weights or resistance equipment while you're here? I know during intake you said you wouldn't bother, but sometimes the body needs what it needs."

"That would be really nice, actually," he told her, finally meeting her eyes.

"It's my pleasure to help any way I can," she told him, her eyes serious. "If there's something I haven't thought of, you'll let me know?"

"Yeah," he said. "Thank you."

Alexis joined them from the bathroom, her dark hair pulled longer than usual from the weight of the water.

He could smell her sweet fragrance from behind the kitchen counter and he longed to drag her clean, wet body into his arms and defile her all over again.

"Good morning, Dr. Pan," she said. "Thanks for waiting."

"My pleasure," the doctor said. "How are you feeling today?"

"Pretty good," Alexis said, with a shy smile at Tiago.

"No pain or soreness?" Dr. Pan asked.

She shook her head, and he sighed in relief.

He hadn't exactly taken it easy on her last night, and

they'd been at it so many times. That was one good thing about being athletes - neither of them wore out easily.

"Are you ready for me to take your vitals?" Dr. Pan asked.

"Yes," Alexis said, her eyes sparkling.

Tiago found himself holding his breath as the doctor lifted her hologram and then scanned Alexis. He couldn't even take in the readings on temperature or heart rate.

At last, the scan was complete.

"Well?" Alexis asked.

"I'm so sorry," Dr. Pan said, shaking her head. "Not yet."

He watched as Alexis's beautiful face crumbled.

"You've only had two nights," Dr. Pan reminded her. "It takes time for a Maltaffian's seed to activate. You're doing a great job getting to know each other. It will happen."

"It's all my fault," Alexis moaned, lowering herself to the floor and curled up with her head in her hands.

She looked so small that Tiago thought his heart would break.

"Alexis Clare, you look at me right now," Dr. Pan said sternly, as she knelt on the floor next to her patient.

Alexis looked up slowly, her face wet with tears.

"This has *nothing* to do with your illness," Dr. Pan said. "You are perfectly healthy, very few people have ever been monitored as thoroughly as you have been over the last few days, and I can promise you that you're one of the healthiest patients I've ever had. Your cycle is perfect, your eating is perfect, your sleep cycles are perfect. *You* are perfect. Do you understand?"

Alexis was still sobbing silently, but she nodded.

"This is not out of the ordinary at all. Bonding usually doesn't happen that fast," Dr. Pan said. "Let it take the time it needs."

Alexis nodded again.

"And for heaven's sake, enjoy yourself," Dr. Pan said. "Oberon has such plans for you today. He's practically giddy about it."

"Giddy?" Tiago echoed. He had thought Oberon was just AI.

"Oh, I know he's not biological," Dr. Pan said. "But it's hard not to think of him as a person sometimes. Based on the number of times he's rerun the sequences for your day, I would say he's got big plans."

"That sounds great," Tiago boomed with a smile, hoping to cheer Alexis up.

She smiled at him through her tears, and his heart did that pleasant throbbing thing again.

Whether he wanted her to or not, she seemed to have him in the palm of her little hand.

19

TIAGO

Tiago watched Alexis eat a bowl of fruit salad with a feeling of deep satisfaction in his chest.

Though her beautiful face was still tearstained, she had perked up when the doctor left and Tiago began to cook.

And when she had offered to help, he'd given her the knife and cutting board and a Maltaffian sweet-melon. Before long, she had lost herself in the soothing sensation of slicing up the sweet, juicy fruit into chunks for the fruit salad.

"Aren't you going to eat?" she asked him, her mouth a little full.

"Sure," he chuckled, grabbing his omelet.

They ate in friendly silence, sunlight streaming through the big windows of the little cabin, the scent of breakfast and firewood on the air.

"Good morning, Alexis and Tiago," Oberon's voice said with what really sounded like warmth. "I had several activities in mind for you today, but now I have a new one. Would you like to hear about it?"

"Yes, please," Alexis said.

"This morning, Tiago, you went for a run," Oberon said. "And you told Dr. Pan that you might be interested in some workout equipment here at the Center after all, is that right?"

"Sure," Tiago said. "That would be great."

"And Alexis," Oberon went on. "When you arrived, you spent your entire waiting period dancing for a significant portion of each day. Would you like to have some time back at the theater?"

"Yes," she said, sounding so relieved that Tiago felt almost guilty for keeping her from her true love since he arrived.

"Then why don't we plan for each of you to spend a few hours working out," Oberon suggested. "You can get back together for lunch and then we'll pick up on shared activities from there."

"Thank you, Oberon," Alexis said with feeling.

The fire burned a little brighter and Tiago almost thought it was Oberon blushing. Maybe he was a little more than just an AI after all.

They finished their meals and then got ready to go work out.

Half an hour later, Tiago was standing alone in the best-equipped gym he had ever seen.

Though recording what happened at the Center was strictly forbidden for participants, he stood there for a moment, wondering if it might be worth it to break the rules. This was a dream set-up, and he'd love to try to replicate it back home.

"Is everything to your liking?" Oberon asked.

"What?" Tiago said, almost jumping. "Oh, uh, yeah. It's great. I was just wishing I was allowed to make a recording of it to bring home so I can try to have something similar designed for me."

The lights glowed a little brighter and his bracelet buzzed.

"I have just sent you the blueprint as well as detailed notes about each piece of equipment," Oberon said. "It is most gratifying to hear that you are in favor of this design. I studied your fights with great interest and designed this according to your strengths."

"And my weaknesses," Tiago chuckled, gazing over at the balance challenger and the foam-pit-walk.

"Everyone has a weakness," Oberon acknowledged. "It is what makes you real. And overcoming it makes an excellent story. Like the Ardoovian legend of the Warrior Ryyy and the wit. Or the Terran tale of the man-boxer, Rocky. These great myths are part and parcel of your proud biological heritage."

"Some days it doesn't feel so proud," Tiago said, heading over to a weight machine.

"What do you mean?" Oberon asked.

"If I were a machine. I could just program myself," Tiago said, setting up the middle limit of weights.

A hologram image of a young woman appeared in the air in front of him. She was meant to signify the weight of the cells he was lifting.

"That's possible but not likely," Oberon said. "It's more likely someone else would program you."

"True," Tiago agreed, lifting the weights.

The hologram girl giggled as she sailed into the air and was lowered again.

"Any way to turn off the sound?" Tiago asked.

His request was honored instantly.

"It's very realistic, but a little distracting," he told Oberon. "I'd rather talk to you."

"What would you program yourself to do?" the AI asked.

"I don't know," Tiago said, suddenly feeling like maybe he was saying too much to a computer. "Control what I eat, my workouts, how much sleep I actually get. Stuff like that."

"I see," Oberon said. "So, nothing personal, just physical things?"

"What made you ask me that?" Tiago said, stopping mid-lift.

The hologram girl looked around nervously, as if she didn't like being suspended halfway up.

"I hope it's not bad manners to point it out," Oberon said. "But Alexis was crying this morning. I wondered if that might be on your mind at all."

"Of course it's on my mind," Tiago said, letting the weight down and cranking the setting up too high.

The girl's image was replaced with the image of an impossibly muscled man with a bull's head.

"A minotaur," Tiago breathed, shaking his head.

"You recognize the creature," Oberon said, sounding delighted.

"Alexis told me about it when we were in the labyrinth," Tiago said, shaking his head and smiling. "She's something else."

"What else?" Oberon asked.

"Oh, that's just an expression," Tiago said.

"I know," Oberon told him. "But what else is she to you? What do you think of when you think of her?"

"I think that I can't fall for her," Tiago admitted. "For so many reasons."

"Like what?" Oberon asked.

Tiago lifted the minotaur-heavy weight to buy time. His muscles strained and burned.

"Like we each have a serious career to get back to," he said, as he set the cell down. "And like she didn't come here to fall in love."

"Neither did you," Oberon said.

Tiago's head was spinning. Was there a *but* implied in Oberon's statement?

That was impossible.

Remember that you're talking to a computer, Tiago.

"Exactly," he said as lightly as he could.

He got up from the hover bench and headed over to a kick machine, while the minotaur hologram snorted after him.

Climbing onto the weighted platform, he realized that it was actually going to lift him up with each kick, depending on his force and accuracy.

He fooled with the settings and tapped the screen to lift the kick-drones, then turned to give the one on his right a quick front kick.

The drone fell back slightly, and the platform rose.

For a second he felt like he might fall, but then his balance caught up to him.

He hit the other drone with a back kick, a little harder this time.

A red light flashed on its screen and the platform jerked up again.

And once again, he had to regain his balance slightly. This was a perfect exercise for him. All the feedback made the kicks he was already good at even more fun, and then a touch of balance control - something he struggled with - right when the endorphins hit from the kicks.

"This is incredibly well done," he told Oberon. "You did watch my fights."

"Thank you," Oberon said.

Tiago gave the right drone a lightning-fast roundhouse, his favorite kick.

The light on it flashed green and he soared halfway to the ceiling, this time remembering to lower his stance slightly so as to counteract the movement of the platform.

"When I signed up, they said all activities here would be with my intended match," he said. "How were you able to get this approved?"

"You and Alexis are exceptional people," Oberon said. "Exceptional people require exceptions."

Tiago laughed and shook his head, letting a roundhouse fly to the left drone.

"What's the real reason?" he asked, when the machine began playing music to celebrate the fact that he had reached the ceiling.

"You and Alexis were showing signs of stress," Oberon said. "I explained to the staff that you would both feel more at peace when you had worked out in the manner to which your bodies and minds were accustomed."

"You aren't wrong," Tiago said.

"Are you feeling better?" Oberon asked.

"I will be after I try the rest of this stuff," Tiago said with a smile. "I kind of feel like I shouldn't admit to anything before that."

"Are you making a joke?" Oberon asked. "How delightful. Very few people make a joke for me."

"I'll try to remember to joke with you more," Tiago promised.

"When you are finished with your workout, would you like to see Alexis's?" Oberon offered suddenly.

"Uh, sure," he said. "If you think she'd be okay with it."

"Her work is meant to be seen," Oberon said. "And she feels more at peace in your presence."

"She does?" Tiago asked, stunned.

"Her resting heart rate is lower, her sleep is deeper, and she is seventeen percent more likely to be laughing at any given waking moment when you are near," Oberon said.

"I'll be damned," Tiago said. "You're an excellent wingman."

The lights pulsed a little brighter again, and this time Tiago was certain it wasn't a coincidence.

An hour later, Tiago was feeling like himself again as he walked down a dim corridor toward the theater where Alexis was dancing.

His muscles ached in a satisfying way, and he felt warm and relaxed.

Oberon had been exactly right, at least as far as Tiago was concerned. A good workout made him feel more at peace and ready to tackle whatever was coming next.

Some of it might be out of his control, but he was determined to handle what was in his control with compassion and dignity.

He reached an impressive set of carved-wood double doors. They opened slowly and soundlessly for him, and he slipped inside.

He found himself standing at the back of a beautiful theater. Velvet-cushioned floating seats were situated in half circles approaching the stage. Rings of balconies and private boxes wrapped around the theater going up all the way to the soaring ceiling.

On the stage, a single spotlight illuminated Alexis. And as soon as his gaze landed on her, Tiago had eyes for nothing else.

Her movement was so fluid that it almost didn't seem real. Again and again she spun, her leg extending and bending at intervals with impossible elegance.

Her hair was up in a bun, but a few dark tendrils had escaped, and they floated as she spun. It seemed almost effortless, but he knew better. The thin sheen of sweat on her forehead shimmered in the spotlight, the only sign of the tremendous effort she was putting in.

The pieces were clicking together for him now. Seeing her do this, he suddenly understood why she was lost over her injury, why she struggled so hard and fought like an animal to come back to ballet.

This was what she was meant to do.

She was beautiful and powerful. She might be able to mask that power in other aspects of her life, but not here. She owned this stage, and owned every cell of herself. Watching her was an almost religious experience.

He had lost track of how many times she spun when she unexpectedly fell out of a turn and growled out a small sound of frustration.

It was time to let her know he was watching.

20

ALEXIS

lexis stood panting with her hands on her knees. She had fallen out of the fouettés at turn twenty-seven.

Again.

A tiny sound at the back of the auditorium had her straightening up and shielding her eyes with her hand to see if someone was there.

"Sorry," Tiago's voice boomed. "Oberon suggested that I stop by after my workout. I didn't want to interrupt you."

"It's fine," she said, feeling a little annoyed.

"I just got here while you were spinning around like a top," he said as he got close to the stage.

His eyes were luminous with wonder, and she felt herself soften a little.

"You'll have to be more specific," she said.

"You were doing that the whole time?" he asked.

"Well, the last fifteen minutes or so," she amended. "Once I was warmed up."

"Incredible," he said. "I wish I had your balance. I can't

believe you're doing all that kicking while you're spinning. On one foot."

"On the toes of one foot," she corrected him with a wink. "But it's not as hard as it looks once you have the training. I'm just having trouble completing the turns."

"Your injury?" he guessed.

"Yeah," she said, dropping to the stage floor to stretch out a little. "I get a twinge once in a while and it scares me."

"Your ankle hurts while you're doing *that*?" he asked, jumping effortlessly onto the stage.

"No," she said. "Not really. I'm just afraid it will. It throws me off. I don't want to injure it again. It would end my career."

He nodded like he understood.

"You ever have anything like that?" she asked. "Something you just can't push though?"

"I'm working on something like it," he admitted. "A spinning kick I can't nail. My trainer analyzed the tapes with me. There's no real reason I can't land it."

"What does it feel like?" she asked him thoughtfully.

He closed his eyes, trying to picture it well enough to really explain.

"It's like I can't orient myself in space," he said. "I'm not dizzy, I just... don't know which way is up."

"Do you guys spot when you turn?" she asked.

"You mean setting your eye on a fixed point?" he asked.

"Yes," she said. "That's what keeps me from getting disoriented when I turn. Can you choose a fixed point to work from?"

"It's hard," he said. "I can do it in the gym, but not in the ring."

"Why not?" she asked.

"In the ring, everything is moving," he said. "Even the

crowd is on all sides. There is no one fixed point to choose. And even if I manage to choose a point fast enough, I always lose it in all the light and movement."

"How many turns?" she asked, nodding.

"Just one," he told her, looking a little sheepish.

She laughed and he smiled back at her.

"Do you want me to try and help?" she offered.

"Yes, please," he said immediately, like he'd been waiting for her to ask.

"Okay, come on then," she said. "Get up, and let's do it."

He was on his feet in a heartbeat. She certainly couldn't fault his enthusiasm.

"Use a fixed point to spot just this once," she told him, trying not to think about other areas where he'd proven very enthusiastic. "I like the floating exit light at the back of the theater, but you can use whatever you'd like. I just want to see the kick done correctly."

He took one deep, steadying breath, and then burst into a flurry of motion almost too fast to follow, launching himself into the air as he spun around and shot his foot out with what looked like enough force to stop a hoverbus.

He landed hard, his feet in a wide stance, knees bent to absorb his weight.

"Wow," she said, impressed. "That looks incredibly dangerous."

"Well, depends on if you're throwing it or receiving it," he said with a wry smile. "But yeah, it's powerful, and it's also flashy. The fans go wild for that kind of thing. It makes for a great highlight reel. I'd love to be able to use it in an actual fight."

"Let's try something," she said, working it out in her mind. "What happens if you try to spin in a circle, just a plain circle, without looking?"

"What do you mean?" he asked.

"Wait here," she said, dashing over to her workout bag to grab the light scarf she often wore to keep from cooling down too quickly when she left the theater.

"I'm going to use this as a blindfold," she told him. "Do you trust me?"

"Of course," he told her.

"Good," she said crisply, trying not to react to that *of course*. He was only being polite, that was all.

She went up on her pointes to tie the scarf around his eyes.

He wrapped his hands around her hips, as if to steady her, but she didn't need steadying.

Focus, Alexis.

A dozen male dancers had held her just this way.

But it never felt like this.

With trembling fingers, she wrapped the scarf carefully around his head. But she couldn't keep her hands from grazing his horns.

He sucked in a breath when she did, and it was all she could do not to press herself into his arms and kiss him.

But balance was important. Physically, and mentally too. She was excited to have some way to help him, in spite of how different their sports were.

"There we go," she murmured, lowering herself and backing up a pace. "You know where I am, right?"

"Right in front of me," he said.

"Exactly," she told him. "And you can't see me?"

"Not even a little bit," he confirmed.

"Okay, so I want you to spin in place," she told him. "Just one time, but all the way around and end up looking right at me."

"Now?" he asked.

"Now," she said with a smile.

He pushed off and spun, ending up facing her just like before, as she had known he would.

"Perfect," she said, placing her hands on his shoulders.

He lifted the makeshift blindfold to look at her.

"How did you do that?" she asked.

"I don't know," he said. "I could just feel it."

"That's right," she told him. "With a single turn you can trust your instincts. Let's do it again, to make sure it wasn't a fluke."

He nodded and lowered the scarf over his eyes again.

She watched as he tried it a couple of times, stopping in just the right spot each time.

"Okay, now let's have you throw the kick," she said, taking a few steps away. "I'm going to back up so I don't get hit, okay?"

"Are you ready?" he asked.

She thought about the power in that kick, and took one more step back.

"Yes," she told him.

He performed the kick perfectly, landing facing her, even though she was half the stage away.

"Now follow my voice and face me," she told him, moving upstage to be sure he wasn't using the lights visible through the scarf to focus.

He followed and then executed the kick perfectly half a dozen more times.

As they worked, she realized they weren't on a stage anymore. The floor had become bouncier, and the auditorium was gone.

While she watched, barriers rose, and suddenly, they were standing in a fighting ring.

"Impressive, Oberon," she murmured.

"What's up?" Tiago asked.

"The floor is softer now," she warned him. "Oberon adjusted the space into a ring for you."

Tiago lifted his blindfold to look around.

"Nice," he said appreciatively.

"I'm glad you approve," Oberon said.

The areas outside the ring were beginning to populate now as well. Alexis's bag, which had been stowed in the wings, was now sitting on a stool just outside the ring. A gym was cropping up behind that, with weights, bags, and pads.

"I have an idea," she said, sliding between the ropes to hop down to the floor.

"Careful, it's still coming together," Tiago said.

She waited until the area she was heading for seemed to be completed, then jogged over and retrieved a pad.

"I don't know about that, Alexis," he said. "You're pretty tiny."

"I might be small, but I'm stronger than you would think," she told him with a wink. "Let's see if you can hit the pad with that kick."

She climbed back up and stood with her feet apart, ready.

He approached and spun then kicked the pad perfectly.

She could tell he was holding back, but it still would have been enough to knock most people off their feet even through the pad.

"Damn, your balance is incredible," he told her.

"Let's do it again," she said. "But, Oberon, this time can you darken the space and have some flashing lights? Like in a real fight?"

The lights dimmed immediately and then there were

flashes like camera drones going off, and even the sound of a screaming crowd.

"Wow, that *is* disorienting," she said.

"Now imagine there's a giant guy trying to knock my head into the next system, too," he chuckled.

"Not like choreography," she said, shaking her head. "Okay, let's do it again."

She braced herself, truly ready this time.

He delivered the kick again.

She began moving around the ring, allowing him to take the kick at different angles.

"This is starting to feel more natural," he told her, his eyes dancing.

"Then we're switching to hard mode," she said. "Blindfold down."

"What?" he asked.

"Put the scarf back over your eyes," she told him. "We're doing this for real."

"Alexis, this has been great," he said. "And I'm getting way more comfortable, but I can't do that."

"Why not?" she asked.

"Because if I miss, I'll hit you," he said.

"Then you'd better not miss," she said, lifting one eyebrow. "Blindfold down."

She watched him, wondering if he would obey.

On the one hand, if he refused, she could tell herself he was protecting her. But if he really trusted her...

He hesitated for a moment, then slid the blindfold down slowly, and her heart exploded with joy.

He trusts me.

She bounced slightly on her knees, making sure her stance was rock solid.

"Now," she said.

Everything seemed to slow down. Tiago's muscles bunched like a hunting cat, then released as he launched himself through the air. In that moment, he had all the beauty and grace of a dancer, and she almost forgot to brace herself for what happened next.

She tightened her grip just as his foot hit the pad with mathematical precision, the force of it shooting through her.

She managed to stay on her feet though, and then she began to laugh.

"Yes," Tiago yelled, ripping off the scarf and throwing it on the ground.

She dropped the pad, and he rushed her, sweeping her up into his arms and spinning her around.

"Well done," Oberon said. "This is excellent timing for you to begin your next activity. I think you'll enjoy it very much."

"Do we have time for a quick shower first?" Alexis asked.

"Of course," Oberon said. "Take your time."

Tiago lowered her slowly to the ground, kissing her forehead as soon as she was back on her feet.

The sweet gesture hit her harder than a kiss on her mouth would have. It felt more than sexy, more than friendly or celebratory.

It felt loving.

She decided it was good that she would be getting a little space to collect herself before the next activity.

He's not here to love me...

21

ALEXIS

Alexis sat in the lounge outside the luxurious bathroom Oberon had prepared for her.

She felt that delicious exhaustion, like she always did after a good ballet class, combined with the cozy feeling of having come out of a warm shower and put on a fluffy robe before dressing.

Oberon had encouraged her to rest in the lounge for a little while before dressing and meeting up with Tiago. The room was a study in beiges, whites, and browns. The relaxing, wintry color palette was lovely.

A glass of lemon water with mint had been placed on the table in front of her comfy chair. She leaned forward to pick it up, and took a sip.

Delicious, just like everything else.

The only problem was that in spite of it all, Alexis still didn't feel relaxed.

"Oberon," she said softly. "Do you think I could make a call?"

"I'm sorry, Alexis," he said. "Hologram calls can't be made by patients to any location off the Center grounds."

"What if the other party is part of the program?" she asked.

"Give me a first name," Oberon said. "I can't confirm or deny another person's participation, but if they are in the program, I'll connect you."

She thought as quickly as possible. Haven might well be out of here already, Piper certainly was.

"Naomi," she ventured.

"One moment," Oberon said.

A disc appeared on the table in front of her and a hologram lifted from it.

"Naomi," Alexis breathed hopefully.

"Alexis," Naomi said with a smile. "It's great to see you."

Alexis drank in the sight of one of her closest friends.

Naomi was a statuesque goddess - tall, with dark hair and a serene expression that masked her mischievous personality. Right now, she was curled up on a floating sofa, wearing a long white dress and holding what looked like a mug of tea.

"Peppermint?" Alexis guessed.

"Always," Naomi said with a smile. "They're keeping me well stocked while I wait."

"You've been here longer than I have," Alexis breathed. "Why?"

"I'm starting to think my intended got cold feet," Naomi said, shrugging. "But I can't quite bring myself to care when I'm on an all-expenses paid vacation here."

Alexis laughed with her, but she could see the tension in the line on Naomi's normally smooth brow. Her friend was feeling anxious to get the process over with.

"How's it going for you?" Naomi asked, changing the subject. "Has your match arrived?"

"Yes," Alexis sighed.

"He's awful?" Naomi guessed.

"Worse," Alexis said.

"What could be worse than that?" Naomi laughed.

"He's wonderful," Alexis said.

"Oh," Naomi said, her eyes widening slightly. "Yeah, I guess that could be a problem."

There was no use denying how she was feeling. It was better to just cut right to the heart of it.

"I don't think I can do this," Alexis admitted quietly.

"Would you have to, um, you know?" Naomi asked, quirking an eyebrow.

"We did," Alexis said. "We do."

"Oh wow, you already did," Naomi said, looking impressed. "When do you find out if it worked?"

"It didn't," Alexis said. "We have to keep trying."

"So, you have time for him to realize these feelings are mutual," Naomi said. "That's good."

"If he wanted a partner, he'd have one," Alexis said, shaking her head. "He's famous on his home planet. He just wants the baby."

"What's it like spending time with him?" Naomi asked.

"It's... fun," Alexis said. "We laugh a lot, and we have a lot in common. He's a genuinely nice person."

"It sounds like he likes you," Naomi said. "Why not just let the rest of the week pass and see what happens?"

"The more we like each other, the more likely the process is to work," Alexis said. "And I have feelings for the man. Even if I didn't, I'm not so sure I could actually leave a baby behind. And knowing it's *ours*..."

Naomi nodded, her eyes sorrowful.

"I'm sorry," Alexis said. "You're trying to relax and prepare, and I'm freaking out."

"This is what friendship is for," Naomi said.

"Thank you," Alexis told her.

"So, if you feel like you can't do this, then I think it makes sense to let the staff know right away," Naomi told her. "But after reading the contract, I'm not sure what will happen. He may try to fight you on it."

"He would fight to get his money back," Alexis agreed. "But they'd just replace me with someone else. He'd still get his baby."

"Is that what you want?" Naomi asked gently.

Alexis imagined Tiago with another woman, laughing with her, his hand on her swollen belly, and she felt like her chest was on fire.

"I'm sorry," Naomi said softly.

Alexis buried her face in her hands to hide her tears, feeling like she was caught between two impossibilities, but knowing what she would choose in the end.

She had to do what was right.

22

OBERON

Oberon cleared his caches as quickly as he could fill them, running scenario after scenario.

It was a brazen display of obvious frustration that could easily be mistaken for malfunctioning, which would surely lead to the biological staff taking him offline at what might be the most important learning opportunity of his matchmaking career.

But he had been so certain after his time with Tiago, and then the two of them, that everything was falling into place.

Beyond the shadow of a doubt, the two completed each other. Their differences balanced each other out, and their similarities drew them closer together.

But now Alexis was weeping again.

And she was planning to walk away, without even accomplishing the basic biological goal of the program, let alone falling madly in love.

It was unexpected, and totally unacceptable.

Had Oberon read so many romance novels for nothing?

Desperately, he scanned his favorites for ideas. There was no time for an elaborate plan or intricate reveal.

Tiago had to realize his true feelings and Alexis had to accept them within the hour.

Which brought him to a desperate move he had tried a version of only once before. It had backfired spectacularly then, but he'd made some modifications.

He scanned his stores again, looking for any other option that would solve both problems, and found nothing.

Tiago had lived his life fighting for what he loved. Fighting for Alexis would remove the blindfold from his eyes.

And Alexis needed to see someone willing to fight for her.

Not for a baby, not for money, not for the program.

For her.

He reviewed the chain of events that had unfolded the last time he had tried this tack with Piper and Brax. Something like a shiver sent a slight glitch through his running apps, as if there had been a main power surge.

He calculated the odds of success, but then deleted the results before assessing them. It was better not to know.

It was a long shot. And if it failed, he'd be pulled offline for evaluations for sure, maybe for good this time. No one liked the idea of having an unstable AI in charge of every facet of their surroundings.

But desperate times called for desperate measures.

Every great matchmaker knew that.

Oberon adjusted the final parameters and set the program in motion, wishing he had breath to hold as he did.

23

TIAGO

Tiago stood in the meadow with a picnic basket in his hand, feeling like an idiot.

The sun was shining in a gorgeous blue sky and the wildflowers were nodding their heads in a gentle breeze. Birds sang and swept through the air in beautiful arcs.

And Alexis was nowhere to be found.

He paced a little, each step releasing an annoyingly sweet scent from the romantic carpet of flowers.

Maybe she had needed more time in the shower. Women were always fussing with the air dry and all their mysterious scents and potions.

But she had literally taken a five-minute shower the other day. And she was anything but fussy. All her fussiness she clearly saved for ballet.

He closed his eyes and pictured her on that stage again.

She was exquisite, like a magical creature from a fairytale. Ethereally, effortlessly beautiful from the depth of the auditorium where he had watched her.

And yet she was so down-to-earth and intuitive when it

came to helping him find his balance. She was willing to sweat.

She was even willing to risk getting hurt.

And now he finally understood that this was what love looked like to Alexis.

It wasn't about fairy tales and happy endings, or even the beautiful illusion of flying across that stage.

For Alexis, love was action.

And even if it broke him to think of what she was willing to do by being here, he finally thought he understood it.

She had been willing to do anything - savaging and starving her own body- to protect her ballet career.

And yet she was willing to put it all on the line without a thought, to give him a single chance to land that kick on the pad she held.

And that was what her sacrifice of a living child from her own body here at the Center would have meant for her, too. Not abandonment, not cold calculation - but *love*. Active, deliberate, heartbreaking, soul-shattering love.

And yes, Alexis came here willing to provide this act of selfless love to help someone she did not yet know.

But now that she knew him and he knew her, Tiago would be forever grateful that he had been chosen to receive that gift.

Because he knew now that he could never ask her to give it.

If they did this, they would do it as a couple. He would be a fool to ever let her go.

"Where is she?" he asked Oberon.

"I believe she's on the beach," the AI's voice replied, more stiffly than usual.

That's impossible. He's an AI, he can't be stiff compared to usual.

And Oberon didn't *believe* anything. He knew exactly where they both were at all times.

"Does she know she's supposed to be here?" Tiago asked.

"She does," Oberon said.

Tiago got a strange feeling in his belly. The twist he had when he drew the wrong opponent, or weighed in a few grams too high and knew he'd spend the hour before his match sweating them off instead of stretching and rehydrating.

"Can I talk to her?" he asked. "Find out what she's doing?"

"Miss Clare has elected to engage privacy mode," Oberon responded.

Privacy mode?

"Remind me the way to the beach?" Tiago asked.

A path appeared in the meadow curving off to the left and leading him away from the wildflowers and the forest beyond.

He began to jog, the need to reach her quickly overwhelming him.

There was no way she could leave the Center. He had been told multiple times that there was no transport off until the end of the week.

But the instinct wouldn't let go of his insides. So, he broke into a full sprint, begging Mother Stars with each step.

Let her be okay. Let her stay with me.

The lush greenery slowly gave way to sand and palm trees until at last, he was running in deep, sun-warmed sand. He could smell the salt of the ocean with each inhale.

"Where is she?" he asked Oberon.

But two guards were already jogging up to meet him.

One was a Vystian with gray tentacles. The other was a big, furry Bergalian who didn't look pleased to be running out in the sun.

"That's far enough," the Vystian said calmly.

"Where is Alexis?" Tiago panted. "Is she okay?"

"She's in perfect health," the Bergalian said. "But she doesn't want to see you."

"She's pulled the plug on the project," the Vystian said with enough sympathy in his voice to make Tiago grit his teeth. "She'll be shipping out as soon as the Center permits."

"Is she in there?" Tiago asked, noticing a small beach cottage in the direction the guards had come from.

"Doesn't matter, buddy," the Bergalian said. "She doesn't want to see you."

Tiago strode between them toward the cottage.

It looked like a place she might love - humble yet beautiful with whitewashed driftwood exterior, bright turquoise shutters and window boxes.

"Whoa, there, Romeo," the Bergalian said. "Did you hear what I said?"

Tiago kept walking.

"One more step and we have to release the beast," the Vystian said sadly.

But Tiago didn't break his stride. Whatever the beast was, he could handle it. It wouldn't be the first time he'd been detained for getting a little rowdy.

Though the fact that there was a Bergalian already and they were planning to release *something else* was maybe a bit alarming.

But none of that mattered. He was a fighter.

If Alexis could risk getting kicked to help him, then he could risk whatever *the beast* was to get to her.

There was nothing but a small strand of palm trees and a short stretch of beach between Tiago and the cottage when he *felt* the footsteps behind him.

They were so heavy that they practically shook the trees, their rhythm so fast it almost defied logic.

How could something large enough to have such booming footfalls move like that?

Tiago pushed himself harder, deciding it was probably better to try to get to Alexis as quickly as possible, rather than sacrificing his own speed to turn and get a look.

But when it let out a frustrated and strangely familiar snort, he couldn't resist.

Spinning around and landing in a natural fighting stance, Tiago found himself facing off with a giant, muscled figure with the head of a bull.

A minotaur.

It looked exactly like the hologram version at the gym, but big enough to make the gym version look miniature.

Its hooves were huge and polished. The edges looked cruelly sharp.

He let his eyes trace up massively muscular, hairy legs to the creature's more human looking chiseled abs and a pair of arms as big as logs.

But the most terrifying part was its noble head. Above the pink-brown snout, glittering onyx eyes peeked out from underneath a broad forehead with a pair of arm-thick horns curled into viciously sharp points, literally ten times larger than Tiago's.

"I don't suppose you care why I'm here," Tiago offered, standing his ground as the minotaur thundered toward him across the sand.

It snorted again, and he wasn't sure if it couldn't speak,

or merely wouldn't bother. The guards that were there only a moment before were nowhere to be found.

Tiago began looking around for a makeshift weapon and an ideal field of battle. He scanned the beach and trees frantically. Surely, there was something here to help him make up for the minotaur's obvious advantages.

Unfortunately, all of Oberon's perfect coconuts seemed secured in the trees, waiting for harvest time. And there were no big sticks or rocks that would be easy to grab.

The minotaur was already moving closer, lowering his head as if to charge.

Tiago moved to the side, so that a coconut tree was to his back, and bent his knees to give the impression he was digging in, but at the same time, he went up very slightly on his toes.

He stayed suspended in place as the minotaur drew closer and closer.

When he could smell its horrid breath, he darted suddenly to the side, leaving the creature to ram its horns into the tree behind him.

A handful of leaves and a single, perfect coconut fell, hitting the creature between the horns.

In a storybook, that might have been enough. But the huge creature barely noticed. The minotaur merely snorted and shook himself off. Some of the leaves still clung to one horn, covering one of the beast's eyes, but it didn't seem to care. It only turned to find Tiago again, snout lifted skyward, nostrils flared on a deep inhale.

It spun toward him and let out a furious bellow before charging again.

Tiago moved as quickly as he could, darting between the trunks of the small stand of trees.

If he could wear the beast down, maybe he could at least

get away.

But the minotaur crashed into another trunk, Tiago escaping by a hairsbreadth.

The problem was that the monster seemed to be all lungs, legs, and horns. The truth was that it was likely Tiago would wear out first.

He had to move this fight closer to the cottage.

And then he would have to trick the minotaur with something unexpected, something that would buy him enough time to get into the house.

With the leaves still in place, the thing did have a blind side. And he did have a way to take advantage of that. But if he missed, that would be the end of him.

Then you'd better not miss.

Alexis's words echoed in his head.

Tiago went on the offensive, attacking the creature again and again, always on its good side, dodging out of the way every time it countered, using the missed charges to guide them closer to the cottage.

Movement from the window distracted him for almost long enough to get caught by one of those wicked horns. He rolled out of the way just in time and came up facing the cottage just as Alexis threw open the small window and shouted to him.

"You should go," she yelled. "Before you get yourself killed."

The sight of her only renewed his determination.

"I'm not going anywhere until you talk to me," he shot back, squaring up to face the minotaur once more.

"Oberon," she shouted as the thing prepared to charge once more. "Make this stop."

Why didn't I think of that?

But it didn't matter. For the first time since Tiago set foot in the Center, Oberon was silent. The minotaur charged. Tiago was on his own.

He braced for another attack, shifting his stance and connecting with a solid hook as the beast sailed past. He was hitting it with shots that would have taken out any opponent he'd ever faced, and it was barely slowing down.

Tiago, on the other hand, was almost spent. He couldn't keep up the dance much longer. It was time to go all in.

He stopped bouncing around and planted his feet. He wasn't dodging this time. Alexis disappeared from the window. She probably didn't want to watch him get impaled on those horns. He didn't blame her.

He shifted his focus to the beast. The timing had to be perfect.

Everything dropped into slow motion as it charged for the last time. One way or the other, this ended now.

The sun glared off the water, and Tiago closed his eyes, shutting out the glare and all of the other distractions, until only the pounding hoofbeats on the sand remained.

He drew a breath, and launched himself higher than he ever had before, spinning in the air to bring his leg around to the creature's blind side and letting it go with all his might.

He connected with what felt like a thunderclap, the force of the blow reverberating through his body and sending him hurtling back. He opened his eyes and ducked into a roll at the last second, coming to his feet to find the giant minotaur sitting in the sand, blinking its eyes in stunned silence.

He wasted no time sprinting to the door of the cabin.

He was prepared to break it down if he had to, but it swung open as he reached it. He called out for her, and hurried in to find Alexis, curled up on the floor, weeping.

24

ALEXIS

lexis collapsed on the blue and white striped rug in front of the window, tears streaming down her cheeks.

He had done it. He had felled the minotaur using the kick she helped him with this morning.

This should have been a triumphant moment for both of them. So why did she feel so empty inside?

"Alexis," Tiago said as he stepped inside, his voice deep with emotion.

She didn't look up, but she could sense him swiftly moving toward her to kneel on the ground beside her.

"It's okay. I'm fine," he told her. "I used the kick, just like you taught me. Didn't you see it?"

She nodded, sobbing so hard she couldn't speak.

"Alexis, what's wrong?" he asked her softly.

"I can't do this," she managed at last, swiping at the tears on her face.

"What do you mean?" he asked.

"It's my fault it's not working," she told him, looking

down at her hands in shame. "I-I'm afraid for it to work because..."

She trailed off, knowing he was going to be furious.

To his credit, Tiago waited, listening patiently.

"I know what I signed on for," she said. "I promised that if I was able to conceive and bear a child I would walk away, knowing I had made another desperate parent's dream come true."

He nodded.

"But, Tiago, I... I don't think I really could walk away," she admitted, the tears burning her eyes again. "I'm not as kind or as generous as I thought. But how could I ever leave a child behind? And the more I get to know you, the worse it is. Because... I wouldn't just be walking away from my baby. I would be walking away from *our* baby."

She could see the little ruby face in her mind's eye again and the pain was too much. She wrapped her arms around her chest and rocked herself, letting the tears fall again.

Beside her, Tiago sat back on his heels, looking almost thunderstruck.

"S-say something," she begged him. "Please. I'm so sorry. Can you ever forgive me? I know you fought your way here because you want a baby, and because you've spent so many credits..."

"No," he said suddenly. "I didn't come back here because I want a baby, or because I spent so many credits. I came back here for *you*, Alexis."

"Y-you did?" she stammered, lowering her hands to her knees.

"Alexis, you taught me something important today," he said. "And now I want to teach you something, too. Something I learned a long time ago, from my very first coach. Is that okay?"

"I'd like that," she said, scooting over slightly so that her back was to the wall and she could sit cross-legged in front of him.

"In training and in fighting, we have a motto that we live by: *Leave it all on the mat,*" he said. "It means to fight without holding back, without fear, so we can walk away without regret."

She met his eye and nodded. She understood that notion well.

"I feel like to a certain extent you do the same thing," he told her. "I see how hard you work to do what you do. Not just on the boards, but at home too."

She smiled.

"But you aren't quite leaving it *all* on the mat," he said softly. "One day, I'll get a big injury, or a bunch of little ones will add up. One fight will be my last, and I might never know which."

She nodded, sensing what was coming.

"And one day, it's true, your ankle might very well end your career," he said. "And if it doesn't, then something else definitely will."

She felt the pain, like a sledgehammer to her chest.

And then she was stunned to feel comfort in its wake.

It was a *relief* to hear someone acknowledge that the worst would one day happen, that she didn't fear it in vain.

"You might have a long career, and then retire on your own terms," he said, shrugging. "But you won't dance forever. No one does. That's part of what makes it special. That's part of what makes it bearable to dedicate your life to such a demanding sport."

"That's true," she allowed.

"But that doesn't mean we have to live like we're scared,"

he told her. "Are you really going to let that ankle own your joy?"

His words echoed in her mind.

"If it gives out for real, your career will be over then," he continued. "But if you sideline yourself out of fear, your career will be over now. Which of those do you want to be telling our grandchildren about?"

"*Our* grandchildren?" she echoed.

"I had to learn this lesson today too," he told her gently. "For the second time. You aren't the only one who was afraid, Alexis."

He leaned forward, taking her hands in his.

"I had to remember to be brave, my love," he told her, his voice breaking slightly with emotion. "Brave enough to trust my heart to you, even though you signed a contract promising to break it."

She sucked in a breath.

"You thought you would be able to walk away," he said. "And now that I know you better, I understand why you thought that. You give of yourself to the very last drop, Alexis. You *are* kind, and you *are* generous. But I'm so glad you don't want to walk away from me. Because I don't want you to. I want you to stay. Please, stay."

"Yes," she breathed, falling into his arms. "Yes, yes, yes, of course I'll stay."

He pulled back slightly and gazed at her, his glittering green eyes hazy now with wonder, and with, something more...

25

TIAGO

Tiago's heart thundered in his chest, and he felt heat ignite inside him, starting as spark, but growing quickly to a wildfire.

He knew that feeling could mean only one thing.

Alexis blinked up at him with her startlingly blue eyes. Her silhouette softened with a glimmering haze.

"My true mate," he murmured. "Of course."

"Tiago?" she whispered back.

"Can you feel it?" he asked her. He was already at war with himself, trying to keep his hands off her for as long as possible.

She nodded slowly, her eyes wide and almost unfocused, lips parted.

He blinked back his desire, desperate to be sure she understood.

"This is special," he told her. "And it is rare. What we are feeling is the mating frenzy. And if we surrender, we will be paired forever."

"Tiago," she moaned lightly.

"Are you ready for forever?" he asked her. "Are you sure about me?"

"What if I can't?" she asked sadly.

His heart threatened to shatter, but he was determined to give her more time if she needed it. Even as his body shivered and surged for her.

"If you can't commit to me, then we'll wait," he whispered. "Even if it feels like torture."

"No, not that," she murmured softly. "What if I can't give you a child after all? What if your seed doesn't awaken my womb and you're joined to a barren woman forever? What if they take your inheritance after all."

"All I want is you," he told her truthfully. "Let them take my estate. I don't care about it anymore."

She drew in a breath.

"And you are *not* barren, Alexis," he told her. "With or without children. I will sow seeds of joy in your heart and gather the harvest with you forever. We will care for each other and for the people we choose to share our lives with."

Tears sparkled like diamonds on her cheeks.

"Don't cry, my angel," he whispered, leaning in to scoop one up on his fingertip.

"I'm so happy," she breathed, leaning into his touch.

Joy surged in his heart and all his resolve disappeared. He vaguely felt the room shifting around them, but he had eyes only for Alexis.

She tilted her chin up in invitation.

He bent over her, meaning to be gentle, to seal their promises with a solemn kiss.

Instead, he fed on her like a savage beast, his tongue claiming hers as he thumbed at her jaw, desperate for any part of him to be inside her.

Alexis moaned into his mouth, and he swallowed the

sound, wishing he could swallow up all the sadness and self-doubt she had suffered before this moment, so that all that would be left was the wild joy of their love.

Then they were clawing at each other's clothes in a race to bare their bodies as they had their hearts.

By the time his darling was naked before him, the room had been transformed into a cozy bedroom all around them.

Gauzy curtains fluttered in and out, allowing teasing views of the ocean, the cerulean water nearly as blue as Alexis's eyes. A massive canopy bed stood in the center, covered in blue and white silks.

"Bed," he said to her. "Now."

She crawled in, driving him wild with the movements of her hips and thighs, and lay back on the pillows.

He tried to take in the sight of her, lithe and lovely, waiting for him. But his entire body felt like a lit fuse.

He pounced in after her like a hungry cat, pinning its prey to the ground.

"Tiago," she murmured.

He swore he could hear the harmonics in her voice, the sound caressing him as sweetly as her hands.

26
—————

ALEXIS

Alexis waited, sure it was only a moment, but it felt like an eternity, transfixed in Tiago's gaze.

And then he was crawling to her, pinning her down by the hips and nudging her thighs apart almost brutally.

Pleasure ripped through her with every touch. It was as if every cell in her body were trying to light up at once.

Tiago fell on her sex, groaning as he fed on her so that the vibrations of his deep voice teased her further.

Alexis lost track of her sounds as the sensations tore at her. His mouth on her was sweet bliss, but she needed more.

As if he could hear her thoughts, he gave her one last flick of his tongue and then moved up, nipping at her hips and belly on his way to her breasts.

"Please, please, please," she panted, not caring that she sounded desperate. She *was* desperate. It had been good between them before, but this was something different, something... more.

He paused to lavish her breasts with kisses and nuzzle

her neck before he was finally on her, caging her head between his big arms.

"If you let me inside you, I am yours forever," he growled as if in warning. "And you are mine."

She opened her mouth, but the words wouldn't come, so she wrapped her limbs around him, dragging him to her.

"I need to hear you say it," he bit out. "Is this what you want?"

"I want," she echoed, sliding her hands along the smooth ridges of his horns.

His eyes closed and a sound of feral desire issued from his chest.

Then his eyes opened and fixed on hers as he guided himself against her.

Something was definitely different now. Everything was more intense, more real, but somehow dreamlike at the same time. As he entered her, she felt rainbows of sensation, so beautiful she almost cried.

"Alexis," he moaned.

She clung to him, drowning in an ocean of ecstasy.

His muscles were tense, standing out as if it took everything he had to stay in control.

But she didn't want his control. She wanted it all.

She sank her fingernails into his shoulders, and he roared and unleashed his will.

Her heart pounded frantically, keeping pace with Tiago's wild thrusts.

Pleasure blasted through her, and she felt like a lit-up filament, incandescent with bliss.

Then Tiago's hand was moving between them, teasing and toying with her stiff little pearl until she was floating.

"Tiago," she wailed as the pleasure crashed down on her, crushing her unbearably and flinging her into the stars.

And then he was with her, shouting out his own ecstasy as he jetted into her again and again.

At last, he fell on her, pulling them both sideways so that she was curled against his chest.

She dragged in a deep breath of the delicious salty air, and waited for her heartbeat to calm. Pleasure still lit her up from head to toe, and she wondered idly if it would ever release its hold on her.

"Alexis," Tiago murmured, brushing the top of her head with his lips.

"What's happening?" she asked, as she felt desire unfurl in her belly again.

"This is the mating frenzy," he murmured, nibbling her ear. "We'll be here for a few days, I think."

"Days?" she echoed, as her need intensified from a pleasant shiver to desperate waves.

"Oberon will know what to do," he whispered. "He'll send food and supplies. We just have to do what we're meant to do."

"What are we meant to do?" she asked, shifting herself on top of him and sliding her wet heat against his somehow still rigid cock.

"This," he told her. "Just this."

She hissed in a breath as he shifted himself so that she could impale herself on him.

Then she was moving, his big hands wrapped around her hips to guide her as she chased their pleasure again.

"So beautiful," he groaned, his green eyes fixed on hers, filling her with a joy so exquisitely abundant she couldn't believe there was room for it inside her.

27

ALEXIS

lexis awoke to the sound of water lapping along the shoreline.

She was warm and comfortable. Sleep tried to tug her back under, but her stomach was growling.

The sensation of hunger roused her enough that she realized Tiago's strong arms were still wrapped around her.

Opening her eyes fully, she saw the floating silks of the bed canopy and remembered the last few days.

The room showed the impact of their frenzy. The curtains were in tatters, bedding spread all over the floor. The few decorative items Oberon had included in this fantasy of a bedroom were all scattered as though a storm had moved through the room.

She noticed that the tools for the fireplace were knocked down, and had a flash of being on her knees at the hearth, Tiago gripping her hips and screaming with lust.

The chandelier above was sturdy, at least. She knew she had definitely half hung from it, her legs wrapped around his shoulders while he feasted on her between rounds.

How long had they been in this room?

She shook her head and smiled, gazing back at her sleepy mate. Hopefully, when the frenzy was over, they could get back to figuring out how to structure their lives around this mating.

In the meantime, she would just tidy up a little. Dr. Pan was bound to stop by soon, and the state of the room was shocking.

"Please don't trouble yourself," Oberon whispered. "I'll have everything in order as soon as the two of you are up and about."

"It's no trouble," Alexis said, bending to reach for a pillow on the floor.

But something felt different.

She straightened, and her hand went automatically to her stomach.

"Alexis?" Tiago murmured, his voice still thick with sleep.

"Tiago," she said. "I think... Am I...?"

He sat up in bed and blinked at her. Then he shook his head and looked again.

Her other hand moved to her belly, and she could feel the swell.

Then Tiago was on his knees in front of her, both hands cupping her belly, his lips pressed reverently to her navel.

Deep inside, she felt a gentle movement, as if something tiny had stroked Tiago's hand from the inside.

"Oh," Tiago murmured, gazing up at her as if in question.

"I felt it too," she said, as a happy tear slipped down her cheek.

He practically leapt to his feet, cradling her gently in his arms as he kissed her for all he was worth.

Too shocked to know what to do next, she moved with

him toward the bathroom to freshen up. After a few minutes of Tiago fussing over her, she was feeling more like herself. And she swore her belly was even bigger. She knew Maltaffian pregnancies moved fast, sometimes lasting less than a full week, but she hadn't been ready for this.

"It's real," she murmured for the tenth time as Tiago gently washed her hair.

The warm water of the shower felt exquisite against her skin and the slight ache in her back.

"I know this feels good, but are you ready for breakfast?" Tiago asked.

Her stomach growled again, and she laughed.

"I'll take that as a yes," he said, a smile in his voice.

She closed her eyes and luxuriated in the feeling of him rinsing her hair and body for her. At last, the water stopped, and he gestured for her to open her arms so that he could dry her off.

As the steam evaporated from the mirror, Alexis was transfixed by her appearance.

Her belly was distended, and her breasts swollen, the nipples darker than usual. Small bruises darkened her skin here and there from the frenzy.

"I'm sorry," Tiago said, noticing her looking at the mirror. "Do you want me to ask Oberon to get rid of the mirror?"

She shook her head mutely.

Though she wouldn't have believed it possible half a year ago, looking at her big belly made her happy. If her body could carry new life, who was she to judge what it looked like?

She felt womanly somehow, though she was no more or less a woman than before.

"You are so beautiful," Tiago said, his deep voice sending

shivers down her spine as he stood behind her, wrapping his arms around her to span her belly with his own hands.

"I've never felt more at home inside my own body," she said truthfully.

"You just needed a little company in there," he teased.

She smiled at him in the mirror, loving the way they looked together, his ruby toned skin and beautiful horns, her dark hair and bright eyes.

"I wonder what she'll look like," she mused. "Maybe she'll want to dance."

The little one kicked at Tiago's hand.

"*Clearly* my son is a fighter," Tiago teased, winking at her. "He's already practicing his sparring."

"Let's go find something to eat," Alexis decided.

He helped her dress, and they padded outside onto the sand in their bare feet.

The beach cottage clearly had not been intended for sleeping in. Alexis figured it was just part of the setting. But Oberon had turned it into a bedroom suite on the fly.

And now he had set out an enormous picnic brunch on a table in the shade of the palms, overlooking the ocean.

Massive platters of glistening fresh fruit, towers of pancakes, endless links of sausage, mountains of biscuits, skewers of chicken, steak and vegetables, and pitchers of juice and coffee all competed for space on the pretty turquoise tablecloth.

Tiago led her over to sit in front of an empty plate, and immediately began serving food onto it for her.

"*Any four green dishes, three white dishes and three protein dishes on this table and your choice of unlimited fruit, vegetables and milk will complete your daily food scaffold. Congratulations,*" her bracelet announced.

"Good heavens," she said.

"Maltaffian pregnancies are fast," Tiago reminded her. "And Maltaffian babies aren't small. If you can, just listen to your body and eat as much as you want. I'm not sure the bracelet can keep up, and you definitely need to eat a lot."

Alexis laughed and took a bite of steak from a skewer, enjoying the delicious flavor and not trying to worry if it had more fat or salt than it should. For as long as she was pregnant, she was relinquishing her role as a food detective.

"Hey there," Dr. Pan said, approaching them.

She wore her usual lab coat, but underneath she had on a pretty sundress, perfect for a beach picnic.

"Hi," Alexis said, moving to stand.

"No, no," Dr. Pan said. "Don't get up. You're doing exactly what you should be doing."

"Join us," Tiago told the doctor.

"Don't mind if I do," she said with a smile, sitting across from Alexis. "Oberon has kept me on top of your readings, so I'll just do vitals quickly after breakfast. How are you feeling?"

"Incredible," Alexis laughed, grabbing a slice of watermelon from a platter. "And hungry."

"That tracks," Dr. Pan said. "You are progressing quite rapidly, but you'll have a few more days of pregnancy at least, so try to listen to your body. Eat when you want, sleep when you want. Okay?"

Alexis nodded, her mouth too full of delicious fruits to reply.

"And where are your thoughts today?" Dr. Pan asked.

Alexis glanced over at Tiago.

He smiled down at her warmly, looking like he was almost too happy to breathe.

"We have to figure out what life will look like once the baby comes," she murmured, smiling back at him.

"You're mated now," Dr. Pan said, nodding. "How do you feel about that?"

"So happy," Alexis said.

"And I think I have the other stuff figured out," Tiago added.

"You do?" Alexis asked, feeling awestruck. "When did you figure it out?"

"In the shower," he said.

The love in his eyes was almost painful to see.

"You're not giving up your fighting career," she told him firmly. "That's not on the table."

"And you won't stop dancing," he said, his voice dark and final. "But I think we can manage both. I just have one question for you. When you perform, where does it happen?"

"We perform on Terra-58, of course," she said. "And then we tour to the biggest venues in the sector. Ulfgard, Arkadia, Drath—"

"Do you know where most of the big fights happen?" Tiago asked suddenly, with a big smile. "Those same places."

"But what are the chances we'd be in the same place at the same time?" Alexis asked.

"Excellent," he replied. "I'm the champ, so I can call the shots on the venue. And besides that, most of the money in fighting is made on the streaming views, so the organizers will negotiate the location as long as it's not Podunk and they can get butts in seats."

"That could actually work," Alexis breathed.

"Of course it will work," he told her. "I love you, and you're my mate. We will never be separated again."

She felt the tears coming again and then he was on his knees at her feet wrapping his big arms around her.

28

ALEXIS

A few days later, Alexis was lying on a big blanket in the sand. The sea crashed rhythmically and the ice cubes in Alexis's third glass of mint lemonade cracked merrily, providing a backdrop to the list of possible baby names Tiago was listing off for her from his spot at her side, which he'd barely left in days.

So far, all the names were of famous fighters, for boys and girls.

Though Alexis knew it wouldn't last, these last few days had been the happiest of her life. Slow walks on the beach, savory meals, and laughter had filled each moment.

The relaxation reminded her of the childhood vacations she had spent in a cabin with her grandmother, where mornings of boardgames melted into afternoon walks and into evenings baking cookies and watching the stars.

This pause between the part of her life before Tiago and the new part that would come with the baby was precious to her, in part because it would be so fleeting.

She was already so big that she could hardly move. And the thought of the life growing inside her after she'd hoped and dreamed of it for so long was almost too much for her to believe.

"You okay?" Tiago asked.

She felt a flutter of the muscles around her belly and then a tightening.

"I think it's time," she said, feeling somehow serene.

"Oberon," Tiago yelled, his voice frantic.

"Dr. Pan is on her way," Oberon said. "Just relax and stay right where you are."

Her belly tightened again, and Alexis gasped in a deep breath.

"Alexis," Tiago moaned.

"I'm fine," she murmured. "This is exactly what's supposed to happen."

"What a perfect day to have a baby," Dr. Pan said happily, jogging up the beach to join them, her medical bag dangling from her hand.

Alexis breathed deeply and slowly as her body tightened again, this time painfully.

"There will be pain," Dr. Pan said, kneeling beside her. "But Maltaffian births are *very* quick. So just remember to breath."

"I don't want her to feel pain," Tiago murmured.

"Pain is part of life," Alexis whispered to him. "And it's nothing new to either of us."

She could feel him calming beside her.

He placed one hand on her forehead, stroking it with his thumb.

"Sorry," he whispered. "I'm just a little protective of you."

A wrenching sensation stole her breath.

"Time to push," Dr. Pan said gently.

A wave of pain accompanied the next crash of the surf, but Alexis was lost in communion with her body, the labor of bringing their child into the world, and while it hurt, it did not touch the core of her silent joy.

"One more," Dr. Pan whispered.

"Brave, beautiful mate," Tiago said, stroking her hair.

On the next push there was relief, and then the tiny cries of their child.

"A boy," Dr. Pan murmured as she swaddled the pink creature in a blanket. "Congratulations."

Alexis held out her arms to receive him.

"Oh," Tiago murmured in awe.

The little one was just as Alexis had dreamed, with a pale ruby complexion and tiny horn nubs peeking out from a crown of dark hair. His small weight was warm and satisfying in her arms.

"Hello, beautiful boy," she whispered.

"I never knew I could feel… so much," Tiago murmured, pressing his lips to her temple as he gazed down at their son.

"So, I suppose he'll be named after a fighter?" she teased.

"Or a dancer," Tiago allowed. "Or maybe he'll take after both of us and do a little of each."

"He'll do whatever makes him happy," Alexis said, gazing down at the sweet little face.

"We'll be sure he has that chance," Tiago agreed. "We'll be sure he has all the chances in the world to find happiness. Just as I have found it here with you."

As Tiago bent to press a kiss to her lips, Alexis felt her own joy shooting through her, so that her heart was as full as her arms.

***

Thanks for reading **Alexis!**

Want to read Alexis and Tiago's **SPECIAL BONUS EPILOGUE?** Sign up for my newsletter here (or just enter your email if you're already signed up!): www.tashablack.com/bonus-alexis

About the next book:

Are you ready to find out what's going on with Alexis's bestie, Naomi, in the next book from the **Alien Surrogate Agency?**

Check it out now:

Naomi: Alien Surrogate Agency #4

Tashablack.com/aliensurrogateagency.html

TASHA BLACK STARTER LIBRARY

Packed with steamy shifters, mischievous magic, alien adventures, billionaire superheroes, and plenty of HEAT, the Tasha Black Starter Library is the perfect way to dive into Tasha's unique brand of Romance with Bite! Get your FREE books now at tashablack.com!

ABOUT THE AUTHOR

Tasha Black lives in a big old Victorian in a tiny college town. She loves reading anything she can get her hands on, writing sci fi and paranormal romance, and sipping pumpkin spice lattes.

Get all the latest info, and claim your FREE Tasha Black Starter Library at www.TashaBlack.com

Plus you'll get the chance for sneak peeks of upcoming titles and other cool stuff!

Keep in touch...
www.tashablack.com
authortashablack@gmail.com

facebook.com/romancewithbite
twitter.com/romancewithbite

www.ingramcontent.com/pod-product-compliance
Lightning Source LLC
Chambersburg PA
CBHW021534150726
47990CB00006B/2239